PREY

—————

DARK MASQUE 2

MAGGIE ALABASTER

JO BRADLEY

Cover by Moonstruck Cover Design and Photography

Edited by Lily Luchesi

Proofread by Nora Hogan

CHAPTER ONE

I stood frozen, staring down at it.

The mask.

The mask.

It stared back at me. Taunted me. Dared me to touch it.

It was nothing more than a piece of plastic covered with black and red fabric, a black feather attached to it.

At the same time, it was so much more than that. This was the mask I saw in my nightmares.

In those, dark eyes peered out, watching me. Knowing what I knew. Searching for me in the darkness. The mask sat over a mouth that was now so familiar to me.

A mouth that had kissed me, licked me, and claimed me.

Mannix's mouth.

Now, the mask lay in a drawer, discarded, maybe forgotten. Did he know I'd find it here, or was that an accident?

They didn't know I saw them that night. Mannix, Ice and Ares. They killed a man while I hid in the bushes, watching. They knew someone saw them but one of them—I now realised it was Ice—let me go without seeing me.

It was his words I replayed in my head over and over.

"I could turn on my phone and find you," he said easily. "But where's the fun in that? The thrill of the chase is much more entertaining. Then when I catch you, I'll know I've earned my trophy."

I put a hand over my mouth.

I wanted to scream. I had to force down the urge.

I gave myself to him. Gave him my virginity.

Had he known who I was? How could he? I'd heard their voices and I hadn't known it was them when I met them.

Only, in the back of my mind, in a way I had. I'd recognised them the moment I saw them get out of the car on the day they supposedly arrived in

Dusk Bay. I convinced myself that was really the first time they stepped foot in town after coming home from Brutham Academy. I couldn't prove it wasn't.

Until now.

I sucked in a breath and let it out through pursed lips. I needed to think critically. Calmly. This might not mean what I thought it meant. There had to be thousands of identical masks in Australia alone. They probably sold them in that dollar shop in the mall in Dusk Bay.

If you were going to murder someone, you'd wear something generic, popular. Wouldn't you?

That was rational, but I knew it wasn't true. I had absolutely no doubt in my mind Mannix was the one who cut that man's throat. Ice stabbed him in the eye and joked about writing a book on killing people. Ares held the man in place while they did it.

And me, I was the one who saw it all.

I'd fucked two killers. What would they do to me if they knew I was the one there that night?

I'd be fucked, in a whole different way. A much less pleasant way.

I glanced towards the door. I was supposed to be getting Mannix's bowtie out of the drawer. He was best man at the wedding of his father and my mother. Helen Knight was supposed to marry Leo Cassani in under an hour.

Leo. Did he know what his son was up to?

The chill already curling through me grew.

Mannix worked for Leo. If the killing was anything to do with business, then Leo did know.

And my mother met Leo through work. It explained everything and at the same time, it explained nothing. Why did they kill the man in the first place?

That, I realised, might be a question I'd never get an answer to. I couldn't let them know I saw them. I couldn't stay here either.

I found Mannix's bowtie and snatched it up before slamming the drawer shut.

I hurried over to the room where he and the other guys were getting dressed for the wedding. I barely touched the door to knock when it opened and Ice stuck his head out.

He was still the same, gorgeous, easy-going guy. His hair was tied back in a neat bun and he wore a perfectly tailored suit.

Any other time, I would have melted looking at him.

But now, all I could see was him with his mask

on, stabbing that man in the eye. Him walking towards me in the dark, taunting me.

"Hey Beautiful, you found it?" The smile he gave me was warm, sensual. Like he wanted that one expression to wrap around me and keep me close.

It gave me shivers somewhere between fear and desire.

"Yeah." I held up the bowtie. His fingers brushed against mine as he reached for it.

The touch was barely more than the pressure of a butterfly wing, but it sent a flight of them through my stomach.

"It was right you said it would be." Right next to that mask. If this was a test, I couldn't let on what I found. The bowtie was long enough to fit around my throat. To be pulled tight to cut off my air.

It was suddenly incredibly difficult to breathe.

"You're the best, Beautiful." Ice leaned out further and pressed a lingering kiss to my lips.

Hopefully he'd put my trembling down to nerves over my mother's wedding, or my body's response to his touch. In spite of what I now knew, the kiss was enough to make me wet. A coil of need twisted inside me.

Treacherous body.

"I should let you go and take that to Mannix. I think I'm going to get some air."

Before I could leave he whispered, "I wish I could bury my face between your thighs, rather than getting all dressed up. We can save that for later." He winked and smiled before closing the door.

My body throbbing, I hurried to my room and pulled off my bridesmaid dress. I rolled it up and stuffed it into a draw, then changed into shorts and a t-shirt.

I thought about throwing a few things into a bag, but decided against it. I needed to get the hell out of here and I needed to go *now*.

I grabbed up my phone, card and what little cash I had in my purse and stuffed them into my pockets. I thought about taking my car keys, but dismissed it. A black Porsche Traycan would stand out like an elephant in a mob of roos.

Trying not to look like I was hurrying, I walked down the stairs and skirted around the busy kitchen. Everyone in there was getting ready for the wedding. If they saw me, they wouldn't think twice until later. But the fewer people that saw me, the better.

I slipped out a side door and headed for a small gate toward the back of the house. It was locked, but I knew the code. I keyed it in and hoped like hell it hadn't been changed since Leo told me what it was. For several heart stopping seconds, I waited for an alarm, for people to come running. Something.

Or worse, for the gate to stay stubbornly shut.

The lock clicked agreeably and I was able to push the gate open. Forcing myself to look ahead and not back over my shoulder, I slipped through and shut the gate behind me.

A track and steps directly in front of me led to the beach, but I went the other way, skirting around some massive rocks and stepping carefully along the cliff face.

I saw the drop, and the surf in the corner of my eye. Falling would suck. Landing on the rocks below would suck even harder. I probably wouldn't die, but I'd brake a few bones, and the guys would find me.

Broken bones might not be so bad compared to what they might do to me.

Don't panic, I told myself. *Just because everyone knew but you, isn't a good reason to freak out.* Okay, maybe it was, but I needed to save that for later. When I was away from here.

I made it around the edge safely and headed for the road.

The direct route would have been quicker, but opening the big iron gates wouldn't have gone unnoticed. Especially with everyone on edge after I was followed home from work the other night. The guys had increased security at the house, but now I wondered if it was to protect me or them. If they'd kill, then what else would they do? Killing seemed like a game to Ice. Like something he enjoyed doing. That was as twisted as fuck.

In the distance, someone shouted.

I startled and ducked behind a tree.

It wasn't much of a tree, just one trying to live its best life on the side of a cliff next to the ocean. It was all I had for now.

I waited, frozen in place. Crouched down as low as I could. My heart thundered harder than high tide smashed on the rocks during a storm. I couldn't stop a soft whimper from escaping my lips. Little mouse, Ice called me that night. I felt like one now. A tiny creature running, scared, waiting for the trap to snap around me at any moment. Hapless, helpless prey.

No one came running. No alarms sounded.

I managed to slow my pulse and racing mind. *Chill, Kennedy.*

Whatever or whoever they were shouting at or about, it probably had nothing to do with me. I doubted they even noticed I was gone yet.

Before I stood again, I pulled out my phone and shot off a text.

The answer was almost immediate.

I replied, then put my phone back and kept moving slowly. If I stood on my toes, I could see the road past the long grass. Grass that was tall, but not thick enough.

I trotted to a tree only slightly better than the last one. I grasped the lowest branch and pulled myself up. Sweat slid down my back. It coated my palms, making them slick. They slipped on the next bough, but I climbed higher, to where the leaves were thicker, the branches more solid. I chose one that didn't bend so violently under my weight.

A hand on the trunk, I crouched down and waited.

I didn't have to wait long. A small, faded red hatchback appeared around the bend. It slowed as it neared the gates. It slid past and came to a stop about a hundred metres from the driveway that led to the house.

I dropped out of the tree and landed with a soft thud on the leafy ground. My knees bent to absorb the impact, almost giving out and dumping me hard on my ass. The ground was no gymnastics mat.

I straightened and ran through the grass, hoping

like hell I didn't step on a snake along the way. That wouldn't end well for either of us, especially if it was a brown snake or a death adder. Hard pass.

I reached the road and bolted to the car. I took one, quick look inside and wrenched open the passenger door. I threw myself in and dragged the door behind me.

Charlie pulled the car away from the side of the road. "You're as white as a sheet. Did something happen?"

"Kinda. Thanks for coming. I know you must have been busy but..." I didn't know who else to call. Everyone I cared about, or thought I cared about, was back at the house getting ready for the wedding.

"Your text sounded frantic," he said. "You look like you've seen a ghost. What did those guys do?" Of course he would assume it was them. They had a history of animosity towards him because we worked together. Mannix, in particular, was possessive, and hated the idea of anyone touching me. Which Charlie had, but only in his capacity as gymnastics coach. Mannix hadn't seen it that way.

"I... I'm not really sure." I wasn't ready to talk about it. How did you explain something like that? How did I explain not coming forward and telling the police? What if they killed someone else because I stood by and didn't say anything?

I could have a metric, if figurative, shit ton of blood on my hands.

I pinched the bridge of my nose. This was all so complicated and ugly, and terrifying. I shouldn't have dragged Charlie into this. As soon as we got to town, I'd figure something out. I'd go to the bank, take out all my money, and disappear.

What was Mum going to think? I skipped out on her wedding day. Of all the days.

Should I have stuck around until after that? I could have waited till everyone got drunk and slipped away. Should I ask Charlie to take me back?

Even if I tried, I couldn't get my mouth to say those words. The idea made my blood cold with fear.

I needed time to think and process everything. Around the guys, I was vulnerable, not only to them killing me, but to their touch. The way I felt when Ice kissed me was proof of that. I was scared as hell of him, but at this same time, I wanted to let him touch me and taste me all over. I wanted to feel him sink his cock into my body.

Maybe I was the one who was all kinds of fucked up.

"You don't have to tell me until you're ready,"

Charlie said. "I'll be the model employee and drive you wherever you need to go. Let's start with my place. You can get your thoughts together there."

I couldn't do anything but nod. Right now, I couldn't trust anyone, including myself. And I couldn't trust myself not to tell him everything. The last thing I wanted to do was to get him as involved in this as I was. If that happened, I wasn't sure he'd get out.

Hell, I wasn't sure if *I* could get out.

CHAPTER TWO

Charlie's place was a small townhouse on the other side of Dusk Bay.

"I was meeting up with a friend when you texted. That's why I got there so quick." There was no off-street parking, so he pulled up next to the curb.

"That was lucky," I said. My tone was flat, but I'd spent most of the drive here looking out the back window to see if anyone was following. If they were, they did a better job of it than the driver of the car that followed me home from work the other night. As far as I could tell, all I saw were people going about their daily lives. What the fuck did I know though? I wasn't trained to detect people following me if they didn't want to be detected.

Charlie gave me a long look, but I didn't meet his eyes. I couldn't.

With fake cheer, he killed the engine and said, "This is the place. It's not as nice as the place you came from, but it's a roof over my head."

He pushed his door open and got out.

I checked again before doing the same.

"It's nice," I said politely. It was nothing special, but it was somewhere to be while I got my thoughts back together. For that, I was as grateful as hell. He could have ignored my text altogether. The fact he didn't, showed he had some balls at least.

"Yeah." He looked back down the street too, before he unlocked the door and let us both in.

The worn out front door was a good indication of what the inside would look like. Tired carpet in the living room led to tired linoleum in the small kitchen. Apricot coloured Formica bench tops were the perfect complement to apricot and white tiles with diagonal stripes. The oven looked older than me.

"Look... Thank you for helping me out." I turned to face him. "I know you're no fan of the guys."

If he knew what they did, he might not have helped me at all. If they figured out he helped me, that could put his life at risk. I'd have to figure things out quickly and be gone before that happened. I'd never forgive myself if I had Charlie's blood on my hands. Or anyone else's, for that matter.

"Anything for my boss," he said lightly. "Sit down, I'll make us both a coffee. Apologies in advance for it not being anything fancy." He flashed me a smile and stepped into the kitchen.

"It's okay." I stepped over to the couch which sat under the window, facing a small TV. I perched on the brown cushions and propped my arm on the armrest. It was covered with the same brown fabric, a hint of formerly shiny metal peeking out through a tear near the backrest. Pea green blinds rattled against the window when I sat.

The whole place was a testament to the truth in the belief that if you hang on to something for long enough, it would come back in style. Everything here screamed late-1970s. Some of it was probably worth a small fortune to antique collectors.

My mother would have hated it.

"I'll take any coffee right now." I'd settle for hot chocolate or tea right now too. Although, I could really use a double shot of something a hell of a lot stronger.

He filled up the electric kettle, set it down on the base and flicked it on. He turned and leaned his back against the bench.

"Are you ready to talk about what happened? Did they hurt you?"

"No," I said quickly. "They didn't do anything to me. It's—" I sighed out my nose. "It's complicated."

He looked like he really wished I'd give him more than that, but I couldn't.

What would I say? The guys aren't who I thought they were? We both knew that wouldn't fly. Not really. Apart from the bit about killing people, the guys didn't hold much back. Mannix was every bit as controlling and possessive as he displayed in front of Charlie.

I could honestly not say I was oblivious. I hadn't wanted to believe it. I wasn't ready to admit that, any more than I wanted to admit to liking how Mannix was.

There was something surprisingly hot about a man who knew exactly what he wanted and didn't hold back in telling people that. There was also something very hot about being wanted in the first place. I was used to being the nerdy girl in the corner who no one paid any notice to. To go from that to getting attention from three guys who basically looked like gods was heady.

No wonder I ignored my own instincts.

"It's always going to be complicated with people

like them," Charlie said. "People like us are better off staying away from people like them."

It was easy to say, but doing it...

The kettle whistled and clicked off. He turned away to pour water into two cups. He added milk and sugar, just the way I liked it.

"Thanks." I took the cup he handed me and held it for a while to let it cool. I might have a masochistic streak that included liking controlling men and assholes, but I didn't want to burn my mouth.

He nodded and went to get his own coffee. "Isn't your mother getting married today?"

That was the most conflicting part about all of this.

"Yes, but she doesn't need me there." If she knew everything, like I was certain she did, then I didn't wouldn't feel bad about missing her big day. She could have told me.

Better yet, she could have insisted I stay in Sydney. Far away from Dusk Bay and all the darkness and violence. I had a feeling I hadn't even scratched the surface of what went on here.

"Do you know Reuben Brantley? Or Caleb Brantley?" I blew softly on the surface of my coffee.

"I know *of* them," Charlie said carefully. "If the

rumours are true, they're up to their eyeballs in some shady shit."

That was what I was worried about.

"What kind of shady shit?"

"I dunno," he admitted. "Illegal stuff. Stuff I don't want to know about, because it would shorten my life expectancy. Why? Do you think those guys are involved with them?"

"Maybe." And by that I meant it seemed highly likely. His confirmation also shone a light on my mother and Leo. Men like the Brantleys usually dealt in legal stuff too, to cover their tracks and look legit. For all I knew, Mum was only involved in that.

I remembered what Mannix said about Daisy Lasalle and her boyfriends being friends with the Brantley family. Did that mean they were also into shady shit?

Wait, did that also mean Zeke Brantley, lead singer of my favourite band, Wolf Venom, was also into shady shit? And the drummer, Asher. He was Ric DiMarco's cousin. If Daze and Ric were into shady shit, then Asher might be too. Hell, the whole band might.

Or maybe I was putting sixty-nine and sixty-nine together and getting six hundred and sixty-six. Just because they were related, didn't mean they shared the same interests, much less crimes. I was my mother's daughter and I'd never even had a speeding ticket.

My head spun so hard it hurt. All I was doing right now was jumping to conclusions. What did I do about that though? Should I go back, sit down with my mother and ask her for the truth? Would she give it to me? Would the guys let me leave again if I stepped foot back inside the gates?

Would they let me live, now I knew what I knew? A cold shiver of fear passed right through me. They hadn't given the man they killed any mercy. They wouldn't give me any if they decided I had to die.

My cup shook and I realised I was trembling. I managed to push the fear aside just enough to still my hands. That was all. I was half a thought away from full-blown terror. I should probably get some hair colour, dye my hair, and then get the hell out of Dusk Bay.

I realised my coffee was cool enough to drink and took a sip. I managed not to make a face at the taste. Go me. Since he'd gone out of his way to pick me up, the least I could do was not insult his coffee.

"What are you going to do about the gym?" Charlie asked. "If you're worried about them being into the wrong things, then them buying the gym might be suspect."

There was no, 'might be,' about it. Although the gym was probably one of those legal businesses they liked to have to cover their tracks. If it wasn't, did that mean I was some sort of accessory to something? In situations like these, often ignorance was no excuse. Especially if the guys had the resources to make it look like I was in deeper than I was.

Fuck in a plastic bucket.

On a scale of one to one hundred, how fucked was I? Any hint of suspicion could destroy any chance I ever had of running my own cybersecurity business. Or getting any kind of job working in my field. Or even one making coffee in a small café.

I pinched the bridge of my nose. "I don't know. It's probably the first place they'll look for me. Once they don't find me there..." It might not be safe for Charlie to go back to work, but what else would he do?

"I'll try to figure it out so you can keep it running," I said finally. It wasn't much, but it was all I could do right now. Vague promises were all I could manage.

"I'm sure everything will work out," he said with

more certainty than I had. "Even if they are assholes, they won't want to disappoint the kids."

"I'm sure." I wasn't sure. Not at all.

I didn't think the kids were the guys' reason for buying the gym, or even in their top one hundred of their priorities. If they found out Charlie helped me, they may just as easily blow the entire gym up. That would be an enormous waste of money, but I doubted they'd feel it, in the scheme of things.

"I'm sorry I dragged you into all of this." I regretted the day I stepped foot in the gym and met him. If I hadn't, he and Nicola could have gone on living their lives, never knowing I existed. Charlie should have been the last person I texted to help me out. This could all end so badly for him. For us both.

"I don't mind," he said. "I like you. If it wasn't for those guys, I would have asked you out."

I sighed again, deeper than before. "If it wasn't for them, I might have gone." I didn't think I'd ever have seen Charlie as more than a friend, but a date didn't hurt to find out.

"Of course you would, I'm awesome." He grinned.

His attempt to lighten the mood fell flat. All I could rustle up was a faint half-smile.

"Yeah, you are. You're a nice guy."

He winced. "Nice. You know what they say about nice guys."

"They say they always finish last, but isn't that what a gentleman does anyway?" I asked, joking weakly.

He snapped his fingers.

"That's right. Finishing last is a good thing." He gave me a lopsided grin like he had it all worked out.

I hoped I hadn't encouraged him too much by bringing sex into the conversation. I didn't want him thinking there was any chance of something happening between us.

If I thought about anything intimate, my mind immediately went to Mannix and Ice. Ice in particular, since he was my first. He'd always have a special place in my mind, if not in my life. Both of them, and Ares, changed me. I wasn't sure if that was a good thing.

I thought Charlie might say more or even invite me to find out what it would be like to sleep with him. Thankfully, he didn't. He must have known I'd refuse. I was in no state to fuck, even if I'd do it with him. Basic functions were difficult enough just now.

Instead, he put his empty cup in the kitchen and stepped over to take mine. He set it beside his and came to crouch down in front of me.

"I know you must have had a long day," he said softly. "You're asking yourself all kinds of questions." His eyes searched mine, his gaze laced with genuine, platonic concern. He was a better friend than I deserved right now.

"I hope you get the answers."

Before I realised what he was doing, he grabbed my hand and snapped something over my wrist.

CHAPTER THREE

KENNEDY

What the fuck?

"What the fuck?" I tried to lift my arm, but couldn't. My wrist was handcuffed to the arm of the chair. I tugged against it, but it was locked fast, the chain strong. It was in better condition than anything else in the place. Of course if fucking was.

I hadn't noticed the cuff before. It must have been hidden behind the couch cushions. To be honest, I wasn't looking for anything like that. Not from Charlie. I should have known better than to trust anyone. My track record was zero. To think I'd just finished thinking he was a good guy. A good friend. He was a motherfucker, like the rest of them.

Ugh, Kennedy, you shouldn't be allowed out unsupervised. Look where it gets you.

Angry, that was where it got me. Blazing furious.

I jerked my arm up hard and fast. If I couldn't break the cuffs, maybe I could break the arm of the chair. It didn't budge. Evidently, it was stronger than it looked. There was absolutely no give in it at all.

"You asshole." I kicked out at Charlie. "If you think I'm going to—" I wasn't going to let him touch me. Being restrained didn't mean he could do a damn thing to me. If he so much as took a step closer, I'd kick him in the nuts.

Okay, being angry gave me bravado. The fact was, I was restrained and he was a lot bigger than me. If he wanted to hold me down, he could do it with one hand. I could fight, I *would* fight, but it wasn't a fight I could hope to win.

Don't panic, I told myself. *Whatever you do, don't freak out. That's what guys like him want.*

Icy fingers of fear slid up my spine. An hour ago, I thought dying was the worst thing that could happen to me. Now...

Tears spiked the corners of my eyes.

"I'm not gonna touch you," he said.

Yeah, like I'd buy that. Asshole.

He stepped back and pulled out his phone. He tapped the screen and put it to his ear. After a couple of moments he said, "She's right here. She came straight to me like you said she would."

I blinked away hot tears and stared. What the—

Who the hell was he talking to?

"Don't worry, she's not going anywhere. Yep, I'll see you soon." He slipped his phone back into his pocket.

"What did you do?" I hissed.

"I covered my own ass," he said with an absolute lack of apology. "The minute they realised you were missing, Mannix knew where you'd go. He told me to keep you safe and let him know where you were." He scratched the back of his neck and shrugged. "If I told you sooner, you would have run."

As if that justified any of that. I was right back to dying being the worst thing that might happen to me. The fact he didn't plan to rape me was a small mercy, I supposed. Very small in the scheme of things. I bet his cock was just as small.

Yeah, it was a petty thought, but whatever right now. I was still pissed and scared.

I gritted my teeth and pulled at the handcuff again. "Of course I would have run," I growled. "Do you have any idea what they're capable of?"

"Probably more than you." He sat down in an armchair opposite the couch, but kept his eyes on me.

"After I spotted you on the uneven bars, your dear Mannix paid me a visit. He told me if I touched you again, I'd die choking on my own balls. He wasn't joking."

His mouth twisted to the side. "After you stopped him from firing me, he dropped in again. Him and that Ice guy. He told me he didn't like the way I looked at you, and the way you were nice to me. He said the only reason he was letting me live was because you wanted me to work at the gym."

"And yet, you were quick enough to call him and tell him where I was." I gave up trying to break the armrest, but stayed on alert. What the fuck I'd do was another thing, but I wasn't going to let anyone take me by surprise again.

"You said it yourself, the first place they'd look is at the gym. The second place would be here. How long did you think it would be before they turned up? And how long after that would I still be breathing? What choice did I have?" He almost sounded reasonable.

"You could have ignored my text." I gritted my teeth in frustration. "They would have come looking, but they wouldn't have found me if I wasn't here."

"They would have killed me anyway, to keep me from helping you in the future. The moment you texted me, you dragged me right into the middle of this shit storm. At least this way, I have them grateful to me. That might work in my favour someday."

"You're so fired." I was half tempted to stand up and drag the couch over to him so I could kick the crap out of him. I should have sat in an armchair. They had the same armrests, but I could have picked it up and high-fived him in the face with it.

What was I thinking? I wasn't usually given to violence. Then again, I wasn't usually running from killers either.

Charlie shrugged. "I'd rather be fired than dead. Maybe Mannix will give me a job. Or his father."

"They can give you the perfect job of having your head decorate one of the spikes beside the gate," I said with extra added vindictiveness. "You could serve as a warning to their enemies."

"No wonder you were drawn to those guys." Charlie looked down his nose at me. "You're as blood-thirsty as they are."

"You have no idea," I said softly.

I took several slow breaths to compose myself, then said, "I saw them kill a man. They didn't know I was watching. I didn't even realise it was them until a couple of hours ago. It was dark and their faces were covered. It was..." I shuddered.

"Probably not their first or their last," Charlie finished for me. "That was why you ran? You figured you might be next if they knew?"

"I probably will be, which is why you need to let me go." I tugged at the handcuff again. "Please, before they get here. We could get out of here together."

"And go where?" He almost seemed to be considering it.

"Anywhere," I said. "We have to get out of Dusk Bay first. Unlock this thing and we can go."

Charlie pressed his finger to his top lip and appeared to be thinking. When he lowered his hand, he said, "If I unlock that, what guarantee do I have that you won't cut and run? I'm dead if you leave me behind."

I won't lie, I was thinking exactly that. Maybe kick him in the balls and the way past, but then grab his car keys and bolt.

"I won't," I said, trying to sound as convincing as I could. "We're wasting time. We need to leave now." How much time did we have before the guys turned up? It couldn't be much longer, especially the way Mannix drove.

He shook his head slowly. "No. I think my best bet is to leave you right where you are until those guys arrive. They can decide what to do with you."

I gave him a dark look. Hopefully I conveyed all my loathing to him. I'd hate for him to miss out on knowing how much I thought he sucked right now. Asshole.

"I was wrong, you're not a nice guy. You're a self-serving son of a bitch. I'm not sure I'd even try to stop Mannix or the other guys if they wanted to kill you." Right now, I could happily stand by and cheer.

"If that's supposed to change my mind, it hasn't," Charlie said. He frowned at me. He seemed to be considering something.

"What?" He was giving me the creeps.

"I was just thinking if putting duct tape over your mouth to shut you up would constitute touching you, or if they'd understand." He eyed my mouth speculatively.

I bristled. Being handcuffed was bad enough, I didn't want to be gagged as well. Especially with something as sticky as duct tape. I wasn't due for a waxing, especially on my face.

"It would definitely require touching me," I assured him. I'd scream my head off, but if anyone came running to help me, they'd be sucked into this insanity as well. I didn't want any more blood on my hands. Especially from someone who was actually innocent. If there were such people in this city.

"You didn't look that surprised when I told you about what I saw." Slightly disturbed, but not surprised.

"Dusk Bay is..." He searched for the right words. "Shady shit central. People like Caleb Brantley run the place and him and his family are the worst. If it's illegal, they're doing it. Lots of it. Running guns, extortion, smuggling diamonds, prostitution, human trafficking. And that's just what I can think of, off the top of my head. Everyone in town either knows about it and turns a blind eye, or is involved in it. So when I said they weren't joking about killing me, I meant exactly that. They wouldn't bat an eye. In fact, I wouldn't be surprised if the newly poured concrete in the gym contained the remains of someone."

"And how do you know all of this?" I wasn't even sure I believed half of what he said.

And yet, there was obviously at least several grains of truth in it. Criminals running around a city, getting way with everything from murder to black-mail to fuck knows what else, was nothing new. Why wouldn't it happen here, in Dusk Bay?

He shrugged one shoulder. "I was born and raised here. I went to school with guys like Mannix Cassani, Ice Miller and Ares Turner. I did my best to try to stay out of trouble, but it was inevitable trouble would find me. And it did the moment you walked through the door. But maybe it's not a bad thing. Being a gymnastics coach doesn't pay very well, and honestly, I'm sick of teaching those little shits."

I was starting to feel like an even worse judge of character right about now. Where he was concerned in particular. He'd done a better job of fooling me and hiding the real him from me than Mannix, Ice and Ares put together.

Where they were concerned, I knew there was some capacity for violence, even if I hadn't admitted that fact to myself.

Charlie, he was an asshole, hiding behind the façade of a nice, gentle guy. Judging by the way he was looking at me, if he didn't know the guys would kill him, he'd try something with me. He could have slipped something into my coffee. He could use his bigger size and weight to try to pin me down. Something. If it wasn't for the threat of death, he wouldn't have held back.

The coffee curdled in my stomach and threatened to come back up. In spite of everything, I felt safer with the other guys than I did with this one. They might kill me, but they wouldn't force themselves on me.

Yeah, that wasn't a whole lot of consolation.

"Maybe they'll give you a job as hired muscle," I said. "How do you feel about beating the snot out of people?"

He stiffened slightly. "Whatever it takes. I'm ready to get out of this shit hole." He gestured around him with one hand.

Okay, I got that. This place was tired, dark and depressing. Only one wall was painted white. The others were exposed, dark brown brick. Every one of them sucked in the light and gave back depression in return. The dark carpet was no better. The whole effect was unloved, dated and miserable.

"You live here alone?" The place was big for one person.

He visibly debated whether or not to answer that question. Finally, he nodded. "I have a sister. She's at a friend's house. You didn't think I'd let her stick around with this going on, did you? The moment you texted me, I sent her off to play."

"What would she think of this?" I jerked my head toward the handcuff. "Most people don't keep a handcuff attached to the couch." The bed, yes, but not the couch. Not that I would knock anyone's kink. If this was what got him off, then whatever. As long as he didn't expect me to take part, then I didn't care.

"She knows I'll do anything to take care of her," he said earnestly. "I made that promise to her after our parents died. They wanted to send her to live with our aunt. I had to work my ass off to make sure that didn't happen. We belong together."

This, right here, was the real Charlie. Maybe not the nice guy he made himself out to be, but not a monster either. Just a desperate big brother who wanted to keep his family together when the system wanted to tear them apart. He still sucked.

"Is that what happens to her if you die?" I asked. "She gets sent off to your aunt?"

"She gets sent off to Brisbane. A long way from everything and everyone she knows. She's only eleven. She deserves better than that."

If Dusk Bay was as bad as he said it was, he might be better off to grab his sister and take off to Brisbane, but obviously that wasn't my call. No doubt he would have done that if he thought that was the answer. For some reason, he didn't.

That wasn't really my problem. Any temptation I had to ask was cut off at the knees by a brisk knock on the door.

"Open the fuck up."

CHAPTER FOUR

ICE

Say whatever the fuck you want about me, but never say the Iceman was born yesterday.

I asked Kennedy if she could get Mannix's bowtie for him, because he was a hot mess running around in his underwear, trying to help his father. We've all seen him naked, including most of the staff. He's fucked half of them. For some reason he felt uncomfortable with the idea of Kennedy's mother seeing him in his boxer shorts. Maybe if he didn't wear ones with action heroes on them, he wouldn't feel like he had anything to be embarrassed about.

Whatever though. Me, I preferred to go commando.

Anyway, so I asked her to get that tie, and she was happy to do it, although I was ninety-nine percent sure she'd rather sneak away somewhere with me. Yeah, me too, Beautiful, me too.

When she got back with the tie, her face was white. More so than usual. She looked rattled. Scared even.

I'd like to think she found some of Mannix's old underwear that he hadn't thrown away. Or a pair of used panties from an old girlfriend. Who knows what Mannix keeps in his drawers? For all I know, he had a collection of cocks from his enemies.

I got the impression it wasn't any of those things. Whatever she saw had her spooked.

After I gave Mannix his tie, I waited a few minutes and went to her room.

The door was open, but she wasn't in there. Rationally, I knew she was probably helping her mother.

Not wanting to disturb them and blessed, or cursed, with boundless curiosity, I stepped over to her walk-in wardrobe and took a peek in her top drawer.

I picked up a pair of black, lacy panties and took note of the size. A good boyfriend always knows his girlfriend's underwear size, so he can buy her all the pretty things and get them right. Right?

Stashed in a corner of the drawer, was a small

bottle of perfume. I pulled it out and popped off the lid. I raised it to my nose and inhaled the soft, floral scent. It wasn't Kennedy's usual one, but it was nice enough. Perfume always smelled better on a person than it did in the bottle.

I decided she wouldn't miss it, so I put the lid back on before sliding the bottle into my pocket. I did the same with a pair of white, floral panties. Just in case I forgot her size.

That would be lame, wouldn't it?

I turned around and that was when I noticed a puddle of green in the corner. Her bridesmaid dress. From the look of it, she'd taken it off in a hurry and stuffed it down where she thought no one would see. And no one would have if I wasn't sniffing around her stuff.

I picked it up and smelled it. Definitely a different perfume from the one in the bottle in my pocket.

I shook out the dress and placed it up on a hanger. Kennedy wouldn't want it wrinkled. She must have been in a hurry or she would have thought of that. She wasn't the messy type by nature, as far as I could tell. Her room was always neat, with every-thing put away in its right place.

I organised her hangers so there was a precise

finger space between each one. I used my little finger, because if she wanted to keep everything hanging as tidily as this, she'd have to use her own finger. My little finger might be bigger than any of hers, but it was close enough. I was nothing if not thoughtful.

Once it was done, I stepped back to take a look and nod. Much better.

I thought about taking everything out of her drawers and rearranging them, but figured I'd leave that until she got back. In case she preferred it a different way.

I strolled back over to the room where the other guys were getting changed and stepped inside.

I jerked my head to the side to indicate to Mannix and Ares that I wanted to talk to them. Mannix managed to be wearing suit pants, shoes and his white button down shirt.

Judging by the bulge in his pants pocket, he was leaving his bowtie until the last minute. Or he was happy to see me.

Sadly, since his cock wasn't as slanted as mine, it must be the tie.

Relatable. I hated the things too, even though we looked pretty fucking hot dressed up all fancy. Mannix in particular.

Although, let's be real here, he looks smoking hot in anything. Or nothing.

I once tried to figure out who was hotter between him, Kennedy and Ares. They all did it for me, although I suspected it would only ever be one way with Ares. His loss.

Ares and Mannix both gave me a funny look, but followed me over to the side of the room.

"Kennedy seems to be gone," I said casually.

Mannix was the first to stop staring and speak. "What the fuck? Gone where? Why?"

"My guess is that she saw something she didn't like," I said. "As to where she went—"

My words were interrupted by the sound of Mannix's phone ringing.

He scowled, but snatched it up from the table and put it to his ear.

"What the fuck did you do?"

Apparently that was the new version of 'hello.' People worried about the handwritten letter becoming a lost art form, but maybe they should be concerned about people not knowing how to answer the phone and talk on it. Young people these days.

"Wild guess, that's not Kennedy," Ares remarked.

I snorted softly. That sounded about right. Mannix might have growled at her like that, but he would have called her Princess. He could be sweet when he wanted to.

"Where is she?" Mannix demanded. He shut up long enough to let whoever was on the other end of the line speak.

It sounded like that Charlie guy from the gym. No wonder Mannix was pissed. He'd be lucky not to have his cock added to the cock collection. If that was such a thing.

Honestly, I could picture it now. I could get one of those shadowbox things and hang it on the wall in my workroom. I could pin and label each cock. Of course, I'd have to leave a space or two to imply I was ready to add more to the collection at a moment's notice. I bet that would make people talk much more quickly.

On the other hand, that would spoil my fun. I put that on my mental *maybe* list. I'd revisit it later.

"Take her there and keep her there," Mannix was saying. "We'll be right there. You know what will happen to you if you touch her." He hung up without waiting for a reply.

If that wasn't confirmation speaking on the phone was a dying art form, I didn't know what was.

"That was that Charlie prick. Kennedy texted

him. He's going to pick her up and take her to his place. We're going there to get her. *Now.*"

Leo stepped out of the bathroom in time to hear that last sentence. He adjusted the sleeves of his tuxedo and asked, "Is everything all right?"

"It will be," Mannix said curtly. "We won't be long. Helen probably isn't ready yet anyway."

If Leo was tempted to tell us we couldn't go, Mannix marched out the door before he could.

I glanced at Leo and shrugged before I followed Mannix.

Ares was a few steps behind me, moving with an aura of reluctance. He was still in his, 'pretending to hate Kennedy,' mode. I had no idea who he thought he was fooling. He didn't fool me for a minute. Like I said, the Iceman wasn't born yesterday. Not even the day before that.

We didn't question Mannix when he stomped over to his car and slipped into the driver's seat. There was no point arguing with him most of the time, but not when he was in the mood he was in right now. He was like a hibernating bear who got woken up in the middle of a good dream. Try to get in the way and you may get a claw in your face.

While I didn't mind a few good scratch marks,

and some pain, we didn't have time for that right now. Later though, I was there for it.

Ares climbed into the front passenger seat like he was taking the job of shotgun seriously.

I suspected he liked to pretend he was actually the god of war, but drive-by shootings weren't our style. They were messy, tacky and impersonal. If we went after someone, we wanted them to see us.

Seeing the fear in people's eyes and smelling it on them was almost as arousing as Kennedy. In spite of what the guys thought, I didn't kill my pet rabbit, Mr Flopsy, but I'd killed lots of other things just to see what would happen, and because I enjoyed the way it felt.

People were the most satisfying. Animals had no idea why you were doing it. Humans always did.

For the record, I've never killed a dog. Or a cat. I might be slightly unhinged, but I'm not a monster.

Mannix all but flew his black SUV through the big iron gates and along the streets of Dusk Bay.

I sat sideways across the back seat and enjoyed the ride. His driving was the closest thing to a roller-coaster I could get without going on an actual roller coaster. If he got pulled up and booked as often as regular people, he would have lost his license several times over by now. Typical young male driver.

It was the adrenaline rush I needed right now. The idea that he might lose control at any moment and smash the car into a tree, killing us all. It had yet to happen, obviously, but that didn't lessen the fun.

I leaned my head against the back of the seat and wondered if Mannix would let me pull out Charlie's toenails, one by one. I didn't need his permission, but there was some kind of chain of command when it came to work stuff. Sometimes I didn't listen. Usually I did. In our line of work and lifestyle, not listening tended to shorten our life expectancy.

If Leo ordered Mannix to kill me, he'd have to. I might even let him, as long as he made it interesting.

Better not to let it get to that point though. Death was a bit too permanent for my liking.

"What the hell did you say to her to make her run off?" Mannix asked over his shoulder.

"I asked her to get your bowtie for you," I said. "If I had a clue the experience would be so traumatic, I wouldn't have asked."

Mannix grunted.

"We've all seen Mannix's room," Ares said. "If it doesn't scare people off, nowhere will."

"Fuck off," Mannix growled. "You want to walk the rest of the way to town?"

"No, but it would be safer than your driving,"

Ares said. "We both know we don't have time to stop and drop me off," he added before Mannix could slow down.

Mannix muttered something about investing in ejector seats, and took a corner so fast I'd almost swear the right-hand tires left the road.

I grinned. "Do we have time to go around and do that again?"

For some reason, Mannix ignored me. I guessed he wasn't having as much fun as I was. Shame.

We finally pulled up in front of an address in a less affluent part of the city. I knew I didn't imagine the stiffening of Ares' back. He never liked this part of Dusk Bay, for some reason.

Me, I liked it. It was gritty and real. The people here were regular people. A lot of them worked for us. Those who didn't usually had a fair idea of who we were and why it was a good idea to give us a wide berth. Once in a while they'd give us trouble and try to upset the status quo, but it never lasted very long. A few deaths here and there took care of that.

Good times.

Ares and I walked a couple of steps behind Mannix as he strode up to Charlie's front door. We probably looked like the mafia boss and his under-lings that Mannix aspired to be. Would be some day, when Leo handed over the reins. This was good practice for when that happened.

Mannix hammered on the door so hard I was surprised he didn't knock it in.

"Open the fuck up."

CHAPTER FIVE

KENNEDY

I gave Charlie a last pleading look, which he ignored.

Half an eye on me, he hurried to the door, unlocked and opened it.

Mannix shoved past him and strode inside. He looked way too good in his tuxedo pants and white button down. The fabric was taut over his broad chest and shoulders. His pants were a snug fit, defining the muscles in his thighs.

Ice followed him in, no less panty-melting in his full suit. His shirt was dark grey, but the rest of his outfit was black. He looked mysterious and sleek, in a terrifying kind of way.

Ares followed the others in like an afterthought. He also wore a suit, but his was grey and he wasn't wearing a tie. He looked like he'd come straight from the pages of a magazine. They all did.

While Mannix stopped to give Charlie a dark look, Ice slid past him and came to sit down beside me.

He eyed the handcuff and gave me a knowing smile.

"Well this is interesting."

It shouldn't surprise me his thoughts would immediately be sexual. He was a guy, after all.

My insides might have been trembling, but I managed to raise my chin and stare him down.

"We're not going to hurt you," he said as though he saw right through the brave façade. "No matter what happens, that's the last thing any of us wants."

I held his gaze as long as I could, but I was the first to blink and look away.

Ice placed his knuckle under my chin and turned my face back towards him.

"Hey, Beautiful," he said softly. "It's okay, I promise."

I swallowed, but managed to look him right in his face. I didn't know how, but I got the feeling he knew exactly why I ran. If he did, how could he promise not to hurt me?

"I don't know what the fuck is going on," Mannix

started. "But we're going home. Now." He gestured for Charlie to give him the key to the handcuffs. "We're going to watch our parents get married and then we'll sort this out." His tone left no room for argument.

Charlie walked over to the kitchen and took the key out of the drawer. He handed it to Mannix who tossed it to Ice. Ice caught it with one hand and crouched down to unlock the handcuff from the couch.

I started to jerk my wrist away and stand, but before I could, Ice snapped the cuff around his own wrist.

I dropped back down with a plop.

Fuck.

"I've always wanted to know how it felt to be handcuffed to someone." Ice smiled like he was playing some kind of fun game and not a terrifying one of cat and mouse. I was a tiny mouse and they were the three, hungry lions.

He slipped the key into his pocket and stood, pulling me to my feet in the process.

"This could be fun, don't you think?" He grinned.

"Not as much fun as it would be if you took this off." I raised my hand and looked pointedly at the handcuff.

His mouth curled up further. He leaned in and said, "I'll happily take everything off you but that."

"I can't go to my mother's wedding handcuffed to you, or anyone else," I pointed out.

He looked thoughtful. "It is more of a bachelor party thing, but we'll make it work. Don't worry. It'll be fun."

"Let's go," Mannix said. He nodded at Ares to step out the door first and moved around so he was behind us.

I felt like I was being marched to my execution.

I gave Charlie a dirty look before I reluctantly walked outside. It did nothing to make me feel better. He was still fired. Unless the guys let him manage the place after they did away with me. In spite of Ice's assurances, I couldn't see how this would end any other way. I was a witness to a crime they committed, how could they possibly let me live, even if they gave a shit about me like they claimed to?

Ice opened the back door to the SUV and gave a sweeping gesture for me to climb in first. He followed close behind, his arm outstretched so the chain of the handcuffs was never taut.

"Can you get your seatbelt on?" He genuinely looked concerned for my safety. Maybe he didn't want me ruining his fun later.

"I can manage," I said quickly. I grabbed it and clicked it into place.

Ice did the same with his and said, "Are you comfortable, Beautiful? You look as though you think I'm about to eat you whole."

"Aren't you?" I asked.

He placed a hand on my knee. "If you want me to. I've never gone down on someone in the back of a car while handcuffed to them. I'm guessing you haven't either."

I snorted softly and moved over, away from him. As far as I could get with the fucking handcuff on anyway.

"I'll take that as a no." But his smile faded. The look he gave me all but confirmed I was right. He knew what I saw that night. The congenial, friendly Ice was one of the masks he showed the world. Underneath that was a stone cold killer. A man who took pleasure at sticking a knife in another man's eye, then joking about it.

I swallowed hard.

"I didn't mean to—" I wasn't even sure what I was going to say, but he cut it off with a shake of his head.

"When we get back. We'll talk and you'll under-stand." It didn't sound like he was giving me any choice. Of course he wasn't. He could have unlocked my handcuff and asked me if I wanted to come back with them, but he didn't. Instead, I was restrained like an animal. Or a criminal.

The irony wasn't lost on me.

My mouth moved but no coherent sound came out. I knew the expression on my face clearly said I understood what he was referring to.

Every now and then, Mannix would look back over his shoulder, but he didn't say anything. Neither he nor Ares seemed to have a clue what was going on.

Mannix had gone to Charlie's house to get back what was his. I could only guess at why Ares came along. Presumably because whatever the other guys did, he took part. Or maybe he'd thought he could talk the other guys into leaving me there.

I looked back at Ice.

I should have been more scared of him than I was. More scared of all of them. Rationally, I wasn't getting out of this alive. My heart and body said otherwise. Maybe the message here was to listen to your brain, not the rest of you, but I couldn't help myself. Even now, I wanted all of them. I wanted Ice to tear off my shorts and panties and bury his face between my thighs. I wanted to feel his cock slide into my pussy.

What the fuck was wrong with me? Normal people didn't lust after murderers. Did they? Did I have an actual clue how normal people behaved? I was starting to think I had none. None at all. No wonder I was a terrible judge of character, I couldn't even figure myself out.

"I won't say anything," I said softly.

Ice closed the distance between us. He twisted at what looked like an uncomfortable angle, and put his hand on my shoulder.

"I know you're confused, but you have nothing to worry about. I promise. Let's just get through this wedding and we'll sort everything out."

I wanted to believe him, but I saw what I saw.

There was one thing I needed to know.

"Does my mother know? Does Leo?"

"Leo definitely." Ice nodded. "Your mother, more or less. But don't freak out," he added as I was about to freak out. "Everything will make complete sense. If we had time..." He glanced at the window. "You'll have questions and we want to answer every single one of them."

"Do we?" Ares asked. He glanced over the back of the seat and glared at me. He curled his lip like he wished I was back at Charlie's place. Or anywhere but here.

I looked back at him with the same expression. Did he think I wanted to be here? I wouldn't have run away in the first place if I did. But now I was back, they owed me some kind of explanation.

"Of course we do," Ice said. "Our girl deserves all the answers."

"That depends what the fucking questions are," Ares growled.

"It doesn't matter what the fucking questions are," Mannix snarled. "We'll get this shit figured out and then there will be no more secrets between any of us." Like always, he left no room for argument.

"See?" Ice asked. "There's nothing to be worried about. Except that if we don't hurry, we'll be late. If there's anything Leo hates, it's people who are late."

That didn't bode well for me, since it was my fault they were late. Well, in as much as they felt the need to come and get me. They could have stayed back at the house and come for me afterwards. Or not at all.

This hole I was in seemed to get deeper and deeper.

"We'll get there in time," Mannix declared. He gunned the engine and the SUV flew down the road. He swerved around a couple of smaller vehicles, and took a corner like he was driving a racecar.

How the hell we didn't crash, I didn't know. Maybe that was how they were going to kill me. We'd all end up in a fireball, all of us together.

We skidded to a stop outside the iron gates.

The way they opened was both slow and ominous. The feeling I was going to my execution got stronger.

I should have tried harder to run after Ice unlocked the handcuff from the couch. When he didn't unlock the one from my wrist, I should have realised he intended something. I let fear and my feelings for these guys get in the way. Since those two things were in direct conflict with each other, it was no wonder I was caught out.

"You're shaking," Ice said in my ear. "If it wasn't your mother's wedding, I'd take you away and get straight to the part where we enjoy being handcuffed together."

His words should *not* have sent heat through my body. They definitely shouldn't have made me wet. They should have horrified me. What was happening to me? Had I been hit in the head and forgot about it? Because these thoughts were not normal. Not even close.

"Is that before or after you explain everything?" I found myself asking.

"I think after would be best," he said. "I don't think I could perform with you looking at me like that. Like you're not sure of me. Not sure if you can trust me." He looked like he wanted to say more, but he didn't. I presumed that was part of the conversation later.

Mannix drove the car through the gates and they clanged shut behind us.

The moment they met, it was difficult to breathe. It was like metal meeting metal cut off my oxygen. Like the full weight of the gates pressed down on my lungs.

Mannix parked the car in the garage and Ice helped me out.

Mannix gave me a long, unreadable look before he led us back toward the house.

CHAPTER SIX

"The gate code has been changed," Mannix said. "I need to get my jacket and tie on and see if Dad is ready. Ice, take that handcuff off her. Help her get changed into her bridesmaid dress. Don't get distracted."

Clearly he saw the way Ice looked at me. Like maybe the wedding could go ahead without us. That maybe people wouldn't notice if we didn't show. As if somehow I could think about anything like fucking right now.

All I felt at this moment was trapped, confused, and worried about what Mum and Leo would say. After the conversation the other day where Mum threatened to keep me away from the guys, things were a little tense between them. If she blamed them for me taking off, the situation could get a whole shit load worse.

What was that quote about tangled webs? This one was getting tangled tighter and tighter. The more I struggled against the strands, the worse it got.

"Ares, stand guard," Mannix snapped before he left the room.

Ares glared after his back, but closed the door and stood in front of it, arms crossed over his chest.

I tried my best to ignore him, because the aura of dominance and masculinity rolled off him in heavy waves. I wanted to drink it in; at the same time, I wanted to punch him.

Ice looked regretful, but took the key out of his pocket and unlocked his handcuff, then mine. He pushed both of them into his pocket and smiled.

"Something for later." He waved in the direction of my walk-in wardrobe. "I tidied up in there a bit for you. I'm sure you'll like it." He wasn't even slightly apologetic for going through my stuff. Why was he even in there at all? Maybe I was better off not knowing.

"Um, thanks." Okay, everything was hung there nicely, but it was so nice it was weird. I grabbed the dress off the hanger and shoved a couple of things apart, and a couple of other things closer together. As acts of defiance went, it was juvenile. Whatever, it made me feel better.

"Turn around." I took the dress off the hanger and held it in one hand.

Both guys looked at me and frowned.

"What?" Ares asked.

"I said, turn around." I made a turning gesture with one raised finger. "I'm getting changed and if you insist on being in the room with me, you can turn around and look the other way. What do you think I'm going to do? Jump out the window?"

"I wouldn't be that lucky." Ares turned around to face the door.

I smirked at his back. I might even have mouthed, "Fuck off." At this point, it couldn't make things much worse for me.

Ice was more reluctant to turn around, but he eventually did.

It took me approximately ten seconds to realise he could see my reflection in the mirror.

I moved deeper into my wardrobe and turned my back. Maybe it was silly. It wasn't as though Ice hadn't seen me naked, but I wanted some control over my existence. Even if it was only this tiny amount.

I stepped back into the dress and pulled the straps over my shoulders.

"Can you zip me up?" I tried to do it myself, but couldn't quite reach.

"Do I have to keep my eyes closed?" Ice asked. When he turned back around, his face was scrunched up, eyes squeezed tight.

Although he couldn't see it, I shrugged. "Works for me." I put my back to him and watched over my shoulder as he put out his hands, trying to find me.

I guess you can't hunt me down that easily after all, I thought. Although, they'd found me quickly enough at Charlie's house, thanks to that asshole. I made a note to myself that if I ever ran again, I should be a lot less predictable. Maybe even prepared. I couldn't blame myself for not being ready. How could I predict I'd find that mask in Mannix's drawer? I couldn't. The guys had sucked me in, in every way possible. I was so fucked, I wasn't sure there was a way out.

Ice finally bumped into me with his hands and felt around for the zip. His knuckles slid up my back as he did it up.

His cool hand set my skin on fire, all the way from the top of my panties to the back of my neck.

My whole spine wanted to curl around him and never let him go. The rest of me wasn't far behind.

"You want me to take it back off again, don't you?" His breath caressed my ear and his words massaged the rest of me, sending tingles all the way down to my toes. "You want me to run my tongue all the way from your throat, over your nipples and down to your clit."

I hated the way my breath hitched.

He laughed softly in response. "I thought so. I want to do that to you. And a lot more things too. All the things. Remember how my cock felt deep inside you? How my magic cross made you feel? How my cum was sticky against your thighs when I slid out of you."

I didn't realise he put his arms around me until his feather light touch danced across my chest. He teased the top of my dress down and pressed two fingers inside, one on either side of one of my nipples. He slid them up and down slowly until my traitorous nipples pebbled hard. My breath caught in my throat. This was so wrong, but I wanted more. So much more.

"Ares, how long do we have until the ceremony?" Ice asked over his shoulder.

Ares had turned back around, and now said, "About ten minutes."

"That's enough time," Ice said. He pulled his hands out of the front of my dress and tugged up my hem.

"What are you—" I wanted to protest, but my blood was on fire. I wanted all the things he talked about. I wanted him, needed him.

"You're going to stand beside your mother while she marries Mannix's father, with my cum trickling down your thighs and sticking to your skin."

Fuck.

No.

Yes.

Please.

He grabbed the top of my panties and tore them off. He bent me over the top of a low chest of drawers.

I leaned on my elbows and lowered my head, sticking my ass out with need. Then his hands were on my clit, fingers inside my pussy. Every movement was deliberate, frantic, needing me to come, driving me hard.

I told myself this was crazy even as I plunged over the edge, stars dancing in front of my eyes. He was one of the three last people in the world who I should be fucking, but the only one I wanted right now. My whole body ached. I'd never before in my life felt so empty, my pussy so hungry.

I rocked back and forth on my elbows, grinding myself against his hand. I tried to remind myself what he did, what I saw that night, but all I knew was here and now. A moment of perfect, exquisite bliss. Hot, wet and irresistible.

In that moment, my body was one hundred percent his, to do whatever he wanted with. He could have asked me to do anything and I would have done it. In this frenzied rush, he owned me.

I was still coming down when I heard him undo his pants and push them down to his hips.

I wanted to plead with him to hurry, to bury himself deep, but I had no words. All I could do was stand with my legs apart a little more, inviting him, insisting.

Then he was slamming into me, urgent, driving hard. I cried out with a combination of pleasure, pain and surprise at suddenly having all of him inside me.

He gripped my hips with bruising fingers and drove harder still.

"Fuck, Beautiful, I'll never get enough of your pussy. It's like it was made just for me. So tight, so perfect. I'm going to come so hard in your beautiful body. You're going to feel me for the rest of the night, aching and dripping."

The tiniest whimper slipped from between my lips and I heard Ares groan. He had once told me not to make sounds like that or he wouldn't be able to keep himself from fucking me. With that in mind, I deliberately did it again. If he was aroused by it, that was his problem. He could have left the room.

"I'm going to come," Ice panted. "I'm going to spill myself into you. I can't wait to spend the rest of the night knowing you're going to feel me between your legs the entire time."

I moaned his name. "I want that," I whispered. "I want you to come inside me."

He promised not to hurt me. This was an extension of that promise. I had no idea if whatever they were going to tell me would make me understand why they did what they did, why they killed someone, but I had this. If they killed me once I told them what I saw, then at least I had this.

Ice grunted and fell still as he came. He made a series of unintelligible sounds that might or might not have been words, then he sagged.

"You are incredible," he whispered. "Just incredible." He stood like that for a minute or two, then slid out of me and tugged my dress back into place.

"How do you feel?"

I pushed myself up off the chest of drawers and stood up straight. "Warm, wet and sticky." I would have liked a shower, but there was no time for that. He'd definitely get his wish. My thighs were quickly smeared with his pearly cum.

He grinned. "Perfect." He patted some of my hair back into place and then offered me his arm. "We should go and watch your mother get married."

Still somewhat wary, I took his arm.

Ares was tucking his cock back into his pants. He disappeared into my bathroom long enough to wash his hands. Shame. He should have left cum on his fingers. Why should I be the only sticky one?

"Liked what you saw?" Ice asked him. "Maybe you should join in next time."

Ares grunted and yanked the door open before stepping out ahead of us.

Ice glanced at me and shrugged. "I guess there wasn't much time." His easy smile tugged at the corners of his mouth.

"I guess not," I said. I hoped this wedding would be over quickly because I needed some answers. Nothing in my life was making sense right now, and it was threatening to drive me crazy.

I'd just knowingly fucked a killer. What did that make me?

The worst part about it was that I'd do it again. Not just with him, but with Mannix as well. And Ares. This whole thing was at least several thousand times fucked up.

"I don't regret what we just did." Ice led me down the stairs and toward the door that led out to the pool.

The sun was starting to set. The whole scene was beautiful. Flowers decorated the space, looking gorgeous and smelling fragrant.

"You shouldn't either," he added.

"That's easy for you to say." Dryness crept into my tone. "You know what's going on."

"If you think about it long enough, you'll realise you do too," he said. "But all of this will be figured out soon enough. When it is, you won't have any regrets or doubts."

"You make it sound so simple."

"It really is simple, but we should stop talking about it now." He looked meaningfully towards some staff as they bustled around the kitchen, finalising a few details.

I wanted to insist we keep talking about it. Did these people have a clue who they were working for?

If they had known, they might have run away screaming. On the other hand, would the guys let them leave? Specifically, would they let them leave alive?

I pressed my lips together when I saw Leo in his tuxedo, Mannix right behind him. They wore matching, unreadable expressions.

CHAPTER SEVEN

KENNEDY

"Do I look all right?" Mum peered into the mirror. She frowned at her reflection, this way and that. She bared her teeth to check for lipstick. There was none there, but she ran her tongue over them anyway.

"You look stunning," I said honestly.

Simple, elegant, ivory silk brushed the top of her heels. Her hair hung past her shoulders in curls that somehow held their shape after all my work putting them in. That was a miracle in itself. Or an entire bottle of hairspray.

She glanced at me and frowned slightly at my own hair. I brushed it quickly and plaited it. That was all I had time for, before Mannix told me she was waiting for me. It was better than the freshly fucked look I'd had before that.

"Are you okay?" she asked. "You looked flushed."

I glanced over her shoulder. The mirror showed my cheeks were pink, brow crinkled, and a slightly wide-eyed expression.

"I'm fine. Just... excited for you." So my hair didn't look freshly fucked, but my face did.

She didn't look like she believed me, but she patted her hair and smiled. "I think we've kept Leo waiting for long enough. We wouldn't want him to think I've changed my mind."

"Yeah, wouldn't want that." I looked away from my reflection and followed her down the stairs in heels so tall I needed to hold onto the bannister to keep from toppling the rest of the way. No one could accuse my mother of choosing practical footwear.

She gave me a nervous smile at the bottom of the stairs, and blew out a breath through pursed lips.

"You've got this," I said, because it seemed like the thing to say.

That earned me a grateful smile, and a nod. "I know, I just can't believe the day here. It feels like I've waited..." She shook her head.

"You haven't changed your mind have you?" I asked teasingly.

"Of course not," she laughed, slightly higher than normal. "Let's do this."

One of the staff hovered, holding a bouquet of flowers in each hand. She handed the smaller one to me, the bigger to Mum.

Red and white roses. They reminded me of blood on pale skin.

A thick green ribbon wound around the stems and poured down my hand, the exact shade of my dress. Whatever else might be said about Leo, he could pick a good shade of green. Thank fuck there was no risk of me dying while wearing pink. It's the little things.

I nodded my thanks and she hurried away. Lucky her, she could escape this chaos.

From hidden speakers out near the pool, music started to play. Some cheesy love song by Mum's favourite singer.

For some reason, she'd said no to my suggestion to walk down the aisle to something by Bliss n Eso. Something about not liking their music. There was no accounting for taste. Especially since she also said no to Wolf Venom, Abbie Hart and Blazing Violet.

"You walk in first," she reminded me. I hadn't even noticed I stopped on the threshold. She must have assumed I was nervous, because she didn't look concerned.

We'd rehearsed all this, but that seemed like

years ago. My whole world changed since this morning, much less yesterday when we ran through every step of the ceremony. Did she know I ran away and the guys brought me back? If I didn't know better, I'd think she was oblivious.

"Right." I gripped the flowers and tried not to grimace at the sticky slickness between my thighs. Ice was right, I was going to feel him there during the whole ceremony. It was equal parts hot and messy. Hopefully no one would wonder too much at my expression. I was just as hopeful the trickle wouldn't reach my feet.

I took a breath and started to walk slowly up the aisle towards Leo and Mannix.

Their faces were expressionless, until Leo saw Mum. Then his face melted into an adoring smile.

If there was anything I was sure of right now, it was that he loved my mother. Honestly, that wasn't a whole lot of consolation, since he was potentially an accessory to at least one murder. Fucked up was putting it mildly.

I dropped my gaze and looked at the long, red carpet I walked up. I couldn't meet Mannix's eyes. Not now. If I did, I might forget I needed answers from him. One heated look and I'd be lost. His all over again. I couldn't let him get to me that easily.

I reached the end of the carpet and stepped aside to let the bride stand beside her groom.

The ceremony itself passed in a blur. I only half listened. Most of the time, I kept my eyes down. Once in a while I glanced up at Mannix, or Ice, who sat in the front row.

Every time I did, they were looking at me. Ice with a smug expression, Mannix with an intense one.

I resisted the urge to speak out when the celebrant asked if anyone objected, but it was a close-run thing. I was sorely tempted to interrupt and demand answers instead.

I bit my tongue, literally, to keep from saying anything.

This would be over soon enough, I told myself over and over.

"Do you have rings?" the celebrant asked, bringing my mind back to the wedding.

"Yeah." Mannix dipped into his pocket and pulled them out. There were no jokes about misplacing them. No pretending to drop them. He handed them to the celebrant and stepped back again.

The celebrant nodded his thanks and gave the rings to the bride and groom.

Mum handed me her bouquet and raised her

hand for Leo to slip an ornate ring on her finger. She slipped a simpler ring onto his.

"You may kiss the bride," the minister told them.

Leo leaned forward and kissed Mum gently. They were both clearly holding back, but neither of them were given to overt PDAs. Thank fuck for small mercies.

Leo pulled away, looked at her and said, "I've never seen anyone so beautiful."

Mannix moved to stand beside me and whispered in my ear, "I have."

I made a face and whispered back, "Yeah? Where is she?"

He slipped his hand into mine. "She's right here."

I wasn't sure if I should pull my hand away or not, but I had the sudden feeling that all eyes were on us.

The least I could do on my mother's wedding day was to not make a scene. At least not in front of the few guests she and Leo invited. Mostly Daisy Lasalle, her boyfriends and a handful of other people Leo worked with.

Just ordinary people to look at them. Friends and family. At some point the lines got blurred, and it was difficult to separate these people from that night. Part of me even wondered if I'd dreamt it.

We quickly signed the register to formally, legally marry Mannix's father to my mother, then the photographer whipped them away for post-wedding photographs.

The staff started to bring out food, and move the chairs, scattering them around the pool area for guests to sit and chat. Or plan more murders, or whatever people like these did.

"This looks like, 'after the wedding,' to me." I gave Mannix a meaningful look. In spite of his assurances, I had no guarantee he would tell me anything. If he didn't, I might be tempted to pick up one of the cocktail forks and stick it in his balls. I might just do that anyway.

Lucky for both of us, he nodded. He gestured for the other guys to join us and led me inside and back up the stairs. We all headed into my room and Ares closed the door behind us.

Ice flopped down on my bed on his stomach, but the rest of us stayed standing.

Mannix crossed his arms over his chest and regarded me for a minute or two. "What do you think you know?"

"It's not what she thinks she knows," Ice said before I could respond. "She saw us kill Eric Parcell." He said it like it was no big deal. Like I saw them do nothing more terrible than walking down the street.

Ares and Mannix both stiffened.

"What the fuck?" Mannix dropped his arms to his sides. His eyes narrowed and he looked at me. Then at Ice. "Bro, what are you talking about?"

"The person who saw us kill Eric," Ice said slowly. "It was Kennedy."

All eyes turned to me.

"You called me little mouse," I whispered. "You said you'd find me." Ice's words had tumbled around in my head over and over, but suddenly I couldn't remember them all. It was as though knowing they did it, my mind wanted, needed, to block it out.

Ice grinned. "And so we did."

"How?" Ares demanded.

"I found the mask Mannix wore that night in his drawer, along with his bowtie," I said. "I thought maybe it was a coincidence, but I panicked and ran. When you came to find me, Ice knew what I saw. That was when I knew it was true."

"So how did Ice know?" Mannix asked Ice.

"With this." Ice dug into his pocket and pulled out a bottle. "She was wearing this perfume that night."

My lips dropped apart when I saw it. "That was

in the bottom of my drawer." He'd gone through my stuff?

"Yeah, and now it's in my hand," Ice said lightly, unapologetically. "You should wear it more often. It smells nice on you. If you had, I would have worked out who you were sooner."

That didn't sound like a good idea to me.

"It would have been easier if we'd worked it out earlier." Mannix took a step towards me.

I took a step back, eye wide, hands raised.

He kept walking until my back hit the wall, then pressed me against it, his chest on mine, thigh holding my legs.

My heart raced. I barely contained a whimper. This was it. He was going to kill me.

He raised his hand and wrapped it around my throat. He applied a slight amount of pressure. A little more.

My head spun. I started to run out of air. Panic rushed through me.

"We're going to explain who and what Eric Parcell was." His breath brushed my cheek.

I was both scared and aroused at the same time.

"And," he continued, "who we are and what we do." His lips brushed over mine, barely more than a touch before he stepped back and undid his tie. He let it hang around his neck and worked at the top couple of buttons of his shirt loose.

"My family is connected to the people who run this city."

I rubbed my throat. I already missed the way the pressure felt. The perfect combination of terrifying and arousing as fuck. Every moment was more conflicting than the last.

"Reuben and Caleb Brantley," I said. When he looked surprised, I added, "Charlie told me. He said they were... Mobsters?" He hadn't said that in so many words, but that was what he implied.

"That's basically accurate," Ice said with a smile.

I frowned. "So your family is connected to the mafia?"

"Not just connected, we're part of it," Ice said. "Mannix's dad is pretty high up. He answers to Ric DiMarco and Hilton Blake. And Daze Lasalle. In turn, they answer to Caleb Brantley. Reuben Brantley is at the top of the food chain."

"And you three answer to Leo." It was a statement not a question.

"For now," Mannix said. "Until I take his place."

"Are you in competition with your brother, Gunnar?" I asked. Talking about all this so casually was surreal, but I needed to know if I was going to get stuck in the middle of a gang war. Wait, was I actually thinking about sticking around?

Yeah, the jury was out on that one.

"No, he's happy to be an enforcer." Mannix looked indifferent.

"An enforcer?" I echoed.

"Yeah, he beats the crap out of people to keep them in line," Ice said. "Although, mostly, he just threatens people. Most of them don't like the idea of having their kneecaps broken, so they do what they're told."

"Right," I said. That wasn't fucked up at all. Only a lot. "Is that what you guys are? Enforcers?"

Mannix bristled, but Ice said, "We do some of that, when we have to. When Leo needs us to. But we have other roles."

"What about this Eric guy?" My head was swimming, but I really wanted to get down to why they killed someone. The rest of it, I'd figure out later.

"He worked for a rival." It was the first time Ares said anything for a while. "He was in town trying to stir up some shit for ages. He'd been told not to."

Ice nodded. "He'd had several warnings to get out of Dusk Bay, but he wore down Leo's patience."

"So because he wouldn't leave, he got killed?"

That seemed like a flimsy excuse to murder someone to me.

"No, he was killed because he was trying to take business from Leo, and because he was harassing some of the girls in town." Ice had an unusually angry expression on his face.

"One night, it went beyond harassment. She spent two weeks in hospital, recovering from what he did to her. Leo called us home from Brutham early to deal with him. He doesn't tolerate men who assault women."

It wasn't difficult to put one and one together, but I wasn't sure if I was getting four or five.

"You killed him because he raped a woman?"

"I wanted to do it slower, starting with his balls, but Mannix over here wouldn't let me." Ice jerked his thumb towards Mannix.

Mannix shrugged. "He deserved a slow, painful death as a message to anyone else who might think about doing that, but we didn't have time. Eric was getting slippery, and harder to pin down. If we'd tried to drag him away, it would have been difficult to do without being seen by someone from the ball. It was difficult enough to get rid of his remains."

I decided against asking for specifics about that. I'd never unhear it.

"If Leo tells you to kill someone, you do it?" I asked tentatively.

"Are you asking if we'd done it before?" Ice cocked his head at me. "Yes, we have, and we've done it since. We think someone is coming after us. Eric was part of it, but it's going to escalate."

"It's them or us." Mannix slipped out of his tuxedo jacket and tossed it over the back of a chair.

I was silent for a long while, trying to process at least part of this. I wasn't sure if it wouldn't be better to leave people like Eric to the police, but I knew the legal system often didn't work in favour of victims. That would leave him free to do it again. So yeah, I got why they did what they did. But that wasn't the whole of it.

"You seemed to enjoy killing him," I said to Ice.

"Ice is fucked in the head," Ares said.

I was starting to figure that out for myself.

"Don't feel bad for his victims," Ares said. "If they're coming after us, they're coming after you too. This goes beyond one thug. This is war."

CHAPTER EIGHT

Their words went around and around in my head for hours while we drank, danced and ate. I tried to act naturally, but everything had changed.

I now had a stepfather and a stepbrother, and knew a lot more about the people around me. Too much, maybe.

I spent some time chatting to Daze like we were old friends. I got the distinct impression she knew a lot more about me than I knew about her. That was undoubtedly true. People like her didn't let other people into their circle without knowing all about them.

I also sensed she was aware I knew more than I had the first time we met. Did someone tell her, or was she that astute? She seemed like the type of person who was good at reading other people.

Me, on the other hand, I was someone who hadn't had to hide before. Not really.

I even danced with Ric, but for only half a dance before Mannix interrupted. He gave Ric a death stare, while smiling at the same time. Apparently there was a fine line between threatening upper management and claiming what's yours. A line Mannix wasn't scared to step on, if not over.

He whisked me away, put his arms around me and spoke into my ear. "Don't make me kill him for touching you."

"Wouldn't you get in trouble for doing that to the boss?" I asked.

He gave me a look like he'd do it anyway, regardless of the consequences.

Oh boy.

"I've been thinking about your punishment," he said. His hands slipped down to my ass. He squeezed my flesh hard enough to hurt.

I winced, but I liked the way it felt. It was his words that concerned me.

"Punishment? I understood why you did what you did. I'm not planning to tell—"

He interrupted me. "I know you're not going to tell anyone. Firstly because of the way it would look to the police if you did. You didn't tell them sooner, and you've been living with us. That makes you an accessory. If we get arrested for it, you'll be arrested alongside us."

That was a cheery fucking thought.

"Secondly," he continued before I could speak, "you're one of us. You got scared. It happens, but you belong here with us. If—*when*, someone like Eric turns up again, you'll be there with us dealing with them, the way we dealt with him." He leaned back just far enough to give me a challenging look.

I felt as though he was looking into my soul. Like he knew there was darkness in me that would speak to the darkness in him.

"I guess so," I said finally. "If it keeps people like that off the streets." After a moment I added, "Was Ares right? Is it really war between you... us, and whoever Eric was working for?"

He looked approvingly at my correction, and nodded. "Whoever followed you home that night, that was part of it. If they caught up to you..." He was obviously thinking murderous thoughts.

My blood filled with ice and I shivered. That night was disconcerting as fuck, but I hadn't thought about what might have happened.

"They could have caught up to you when you ran," Mannix continued. "Charlie is a dickhead, but if someone found you before he did, or someone got to you before we picked you up..." Again with the murderous-thought-face.

"Did it cross your mind to tell me all of this before now?" I asked. "I've been living here for weeks, not knowing any of this." That explained the increased security at the gym, and the way they hated to let me out of their sight. It went beyond being possessive, although that certainly was a big part of it. They were also trying to keep me safe from people even more unscrupulous than they were.

"We were going to tell you when I decided the time was right," he stated. "You forced my hand. Next time, come to me instead of sneaking away."

"I thought there was a good chance I would end up the same way Eric did," I admitted.

He stared at me for a moment, then sighed. "That's why you have nightmares, isn't it? Because of what you saw? Fuck."

"Yeah, and because Ice's words were as scary as hell. I thought you were going to spend your days hunting me down so he could kill me. Would you have killed me if you caught me that night?" Did I want to know the answer to that?

"Only if you worked for them," he said easily.

"Who are they?" If someone was coming after me, then I should know who they were.

"Most likely the Bell family, or someone who works with them and is trying to flex their muscles." He scowled. "They're one of the three most powerful families in Australia. The Bells, the Brantleys and to a lesser extent the Fiorellis. Although, the Fiorellis are too disorganised to get much done. Rumour has it they're fractured, which works perfectly for us. They're less likely to come after us if they can't get their own shit together."

I nodded. "So this is a turf war? Like rival gangs trying to elbow into the space of other gangs?"

"Yeah, kinda, but we're more sophisticated than a pack of street thugs." He'd put his tuxedo jacket back on, but he still had his shirt unbuttoned and his tie hanging around his neck. He looked like the opposite of a street thug. He looked more like a billionaire apprentice. Which was precisely accurate.

"What does that make me?" I raised a perfectly shaped eyebrow at him. Mum and I had spent the morning getting waxed and plucked in all the right places, so I knew I looked somewhat respectable.

He pulled me closer and blew softly on my

earlobe. "It makes you my very fuckable, gorgeous step sister. Who now understands what's at stake."

"I guess I do," I agreed. "What does that mean for me though? Are you going to let me keep running the gym?" Could I do it without Charlie?

"Could I stop you?" he asked.

"You could lock me in behind the gates until I'm old and grey," I said.

"I don't think you would tolerate that for long," he said. "And unless I take every device and computer away from you, you'd find a way to get out. Changing the code will only hold you for so long."

"Damn right." I gave him a short nod. "I like that you care, but I don't need you controlling every little thing I do."

He gave me a look that suggested he'd do that anyway, at least as much as he was able to.

"You can keep running the gym, but I'll be vetting any new staff you hire. And any families who put their kids there. And the kids themselves." He was deadly serious.

"Good, because I don't want to let the kids down." I had some idea how it would feel to have the place close with no warning. For a lot of kids, the gym became a sanctuary away from their regular lives. It wasn't just great exercise, it was a great way to burn off frustration and anxiety. That was one of the things I liked the most about it.

"But once you can pass it on to a manager, Leo agrees there is a role for you in our business." He was blasé about talking about me behind my back.

"Oh really?" It shouldn't surprise me he'd done that. It wouldn't even surprise me if he told me he had the rest of my life planned out. For at least a second or two, while standing beside Mum, I thought he'd tell me he'd arranged for us to get married too. I wouldn't put it past him.

I sure as hell wasn't going to say that out loud, in case he got any ideas. I was definitely *not* ready to get married.

"More and more, we're moving into digital methods to do what we do," he said slowly.

"Cybercrime," I said flatly.

"Something like that," he said, not looking even slightly ruffled. "It wouldn't hurt to have someone like you to keep our rivals from hacking us. If you wanted to take it a little further..."

"Mannix Cassani, are you suggesting I use my degree to become a cyber criminal?" I asked. I wasn't sure if I was amused or offended at the suggestion. "Do I look like a hacker?"

He grinned. "Kennedy Knight, I'm certain you

can be whatever you want to be. You're smart enough to get into any bank in the world and make yourself a billionaire if you wanted to."

"I think you might be giving me a bit too much credit, but thank you." It was one thing to create security systems and another to get past those created by someone else. Although, with the resources Mannix and his family had, I could probably do it with a bit of time.

"What would I do with a billion dollars anyway?" I asked.

"Anything you want," he replied. "Haven't you always wanted a private jet?"

"Not really," I admitted. "I'd prefer a private helicopter. Much easier to take off and land wherever you want."

He looked proud at my answer. "I was thinking luxury travel, and you're thinking quick getaway. You're more suited to this lifestyle than you might have realised."

"I was thinking quick getaway to a tropical island for a holiday, not running away from a crime," I argued.

"It's a fine line," he teased.

"I'm sure it is." I was about to find out, from the sound of it. "And what if I want to stay on this side of the law?" Knowing what they did and agreeing to take part in it were two very different things. Or were they? He was right about me being an accessory. The longer I stuck around with them, the deeper I got into an even more tangled web. The strands of this were stickier than Ice's cum on my thighs.

"Like I said, we could use help keeping our rivals out of our computer systems. If that's all you want to do, then that's all we'll ask of you, but I guarantee once you get a little taste for the illicit, you'll get addicted. Apart from our rivals, no one can touch us. We can do whatever we want, whenever we want, to whomever we want. We can go anywhere in the world and see things other people can only dream of. If you want front row tickets to Wolf Venom, you only have to ask."

"Is this where you tell me you kill people who have front row tickets and take it from them?" I asked. Wait, did I really want to know the answer to that?

He laughed and squeezed my ass a little tighter. "No, they're friends, remember? If it's another band you want to see, we can buy the label and make sure you get all the tickets you want. Or, you can hack in and get them yourself."

He made it all sound so easy and enticing.

I admit, front row tickets to any act, anywhere in the world did sound pretty fucking amazing.

"It's a lot to think about," I said. One minute I was a law-abiding citizen, the next I was contemplating breaking a bunch of laws just so I could go and see some good music. It would take more than a minute or two to decide if that was something I was going to do.

"There's no hurry," he said.

"Did you just study business to work for your father?" I asked.

"That, and so I can work for myself some day," he said. "Ares studied psychology so he can understand our rivals and how to manipulate people into doing what we want."

That was both disturbing and hot as fuck.

"And Ice? Didn't he study forensic pathology?" Did I really want to know about that?

"That's something you should talk to Ice about," Mannix said. "His kind of fucked up is better coming from his mouth than mine."

CHAPTER NINE

ICE

"Have you ever done tequila shots?" I had a bottle of tequila in one hand, some salt and a couple of limes in the other.

Kennedy gave me a dubious look, like I probably deserved, but shook her head.

"That sounds dangerous."

I grinned. "We like dangerous around here." I turned to Mannix and Ares. "Are you guys in?"

Mannix grinned. "If you're talking about what I think you're talking about, I'm definitely in. Let's go."

Ares had his, 'I might dig my heels in,' expression on his face. I don't know if mules are as stubborn as people say they are, but he was definitely worse than one of those.

"You don't have to take part, you can just drink if

you want." Without stopping to see if he answered, I led the way up the stairs to Kennedy's bedroom.

This was fast becoming my favourite part of the house. I wondered if she'd let me move in with her, instead of sleeping in the room across the hall. Maybe I wouldn't ask, I'd just gradually bring more and more of my stuff over here.

How long would it take before the guys cottoned on and tried to do the same thing? The room was big enough. We might need a bigger bed though.

I made a mental note to buy one in the morning.

Ares grumbled something, but followed the rest of us.

"Do we need glasses?" Kennedy asked cutely.

I chuckled. "No need. We have everything we need right here."

She gave me that dubious look again, but shrugged.

I closed the door behind us all and pulled a knife out of my pocket. On that same chest of drawers where I'd fucked Kennedy a few hours ago, I sliced the lime. Fruit isn't as much fun as slicing people, but I took care to make each wedge look pretty and the same thickness as the one before. A guy had to have some pride in his knife skills.

"Let me help you out of that," Mannix said to

Kennedy. He moved around behind her to unzip her dress.

Judging by the expression on her face, she realised what we were suggesting. For a moment, I worried she wouldn't go for it. If she didn't, then we'd just drink.

She gave me a warm, fuzzy feeling inside when she smiled.

Yep, she was down for it. That's our girl.

The moment I finished slicing up the lime, Ares grabbed the bottle of tequila and took a swig. He tipped up the salt shaker, letting a bunch of grains pour out onto his tongue. He snatched a lime wedge and bit down onto it.

"Fuck yeah."

I grinned and took the bottle from his hand. I walked over to the bed where Mannix had already laid Kennedy down.

She watched me carefully as I tipped the tequila bottle, pouring a decent amount into the concave of her belly and her navel.

I sprinkled a line of salt beside it and placed a wedge next to that.

I sat back and smiled. "You're a beautiful work of art."

"Thank you," Mannix said, as if I was talking about him.

I snorted and bent down to lick and suck the tequila off Kennedy's stomach. It tasted even more delicious mixed with her skin.

I smacked my lips, then carefully licked up every grain of salt while she writhed.

"That tickles."

I grinned and picked up the lime wedge with my teeth before biting into it.

Around the wedge I said, "Best tequila shot ever."

Apparently done waiting for his turn, Mannix snatched the bottle from my hand and refilled Kennedy's belly. He had just enough patience to wait while I put down another line of salt and another wedge.

I sat back and watched him lick and suck, and she rolled her hips with the most sensual rhythm I ever saw. She made my cock harder than any of my knives.

"Kennedy's turn," I said. I handed her the bottle, and the salt shaker, along with my best lime wedge.

She looked from me to Mannix and back again, and even glanced at Ares.

"We'd all be receptive, Princess," Mannix said.

He was right. Even Ares would have gone along

with it right now. He looked as caught up in the moment as the rest of us.

Kennedy obviously noticed that, and knew she may regret asking him to do anything he didn't want to do when he was sober.

Finally she said, "Why choose? Can I get another lime wedge?"

"Of course," I said. I stripped off all my clothes on the way to grab one. By the time I got back to the bed, Mannix was also wonderfully naked.

"Both of you lie down," Kennedy said.

With a fair idea of what she wanted to do, we glanced at each other and lay down with enough space between us for her to kneel. Confirming what I suspected, she tipped tequila into Mannix's navel, then mine. With as much care as I had used on her, she sprinkled a line of salt on either of us, then placed a lime wedge beside that.

She looked around for somewhere to put the tequila bottle, but Ares helped out by grabbing it and taking a huge swig. He'd taken off his shirt and tie, but left on his pants. That might not be the wisest course of action for him, because his cock was trying hard to break the zipper apart. Oh well, he could buy more pants.

Kennedy started with me, licking and sucking the tequila from my belly button.

She was right, it did tickle, but I managed to keep still and grinned at her.

She grinned back and licked up the salt before grabbing the lime.

By now, my cock was so hard, he was pointing straight at the ceiling. A glance over at Mannix showed his was doing the same.

While Kennedy licked the tequila from him, I rolled over and lowered my mouth onto his cock.

He groaned.

I had a mouthful of him. Kennedy had a mouthful of lime. Ares had a mouthful of tequila bottle. I guessed that meant everyone was winning.

Kennedy tossed the lime peel aside and crawled down the bed. She stopped with her mouth right in front of my cock.

"I've never..." Her face turned a glorious shade of pink.

I lifted my face off Mannix and said, "There's no wrong way to do it. Just do whatever feels right. I guarantee it will feel amazing."

I went back to sucking and tracing my tongue up and down Mannix's cock, demonstrating one way to blow a guy off.

Her lips were so soft and delightfully tentative at first. It was almost as though she thought my cock would eat her, or she might choke on me.

She started with a series of little licks and kisses, which felt like pure heaven to me. Her hand wandered up so her fingers could lightly touch the base and my balls.

Inspired, I massaged Mannix's balls with one of my hands, while the other lightly traced lines up and down his hip and over his ass. He started to buck into my mouth, slowly at first, then gradually deep down to the back of my throat.

His breath became a series of grunts. Then, so did mine as Kennedy fastened her lips around me and started to suck, and graze her teeth over my sensitive skin.

If I died right now, I would die in absolute, perfect bliss.

I caught a glimpse of Ares. He'd pushed his pants down and had his hand around his thick cock.

I'm not gonna lie, I'd love to know how he'd feel in my mouth. I'd bet anything he was tasty.

Right before he came, Mannix slipped himself out of my mouth. He walked on his knees over behind Kennedy and pried her legs apart with his hands. His cock still glistening, he positioned it outside her pussy, then pressed himself into her body.

She groaned around my cock, but didn't stop sucking.

"Good girl," I told her. "You're so good at this already. I can hardly believe this is your first time sucking a cock. Your mouth and tongue are just perfect." I rolled my hips and half closed my eyes. I wanted to savour every moment of this. To make it last forever. At the same time, I wanted to come down her throat right now.

The sound of Mannix's hips slapping against her ass drove me closer and closer to the edge. Watching him drive into her, his face a mask of concentration, incredible sounds slipping from his mouth... I loved everything about it.

She cried out and ground her hips into the mattress as she came.

I grabbed onto the back of her head, and tangled my fingers in her hair as she took her mouth off my cock. I grabbed my length in one hand and pumped it until I came, squirting my pearly juices all over her cheek and into her hair. Ice cream at its finest.

"I want you to taste it." I slowly, carefully, scraped the side of my finger down her cheek and pressed it into her mouth.

She sucked my finger like a baby animal seeking a teat. This woman was going to kill me with how incredible, curious and willing she was. I had so much to teach her. I knew she'd want to learn all of it. Even the darkest, most disturbing stuff.

"That tastes even better than the shot."

"Next time, I'll put it right in your mouth," I told her. But she did look adorable with strings of cum in her hair.

"Fuck," Mannix grunted. He pounded harder, his balls slapping and slapping against her ass. "This is—"

I never found out what this was, because he stopped talking, thrust frantically into her body and then stilled as he came. He dropped his head back and cried out his nickname for her.

"Beautiful, fucking Princess," he panted.

Well, a variation of his nickname for her. Nothing about that was wrong. She was beautiful, they were fucking and she was definitely a princess. One who was quickly becoming a queen.

He scrunched up his face, trying to make his orgasm last as long as he could, milking himself every drop in her wonderful pussy.

Finally he sagged, panting over her, his face nearly touching her bare back.

Over to the side of the room, Ares was the last to come, his eyes on us.

I watched intently as he pumped his engorged cock. Full of blood, it was red and purple and looked ready to burst. Then it did, exploding a river of cum out over his hand and onto the carpet.

What a waste, I would have drunk that.

Some day.

Then he too sagged, before he grabbed the bottle for another drink.

"I don't know about anyone else, but I could use a shower," he said lightly.

Kennedy touched the side of her face and found her hair all wet. I was getting good at decorating her. I'd have to think of more, interesting ways to do it.

"I could use a shower." I rolled off the bed and onto the floor. "Last one in there has to wash my back." I noticed neither Kennedy nor Mannix rushed. If they both wanted to be last, I was one hundred percent okay with that. In fact, they could both wash my back at the same time if they wanted to.

And then maybe I could fuck one or both of them again.

CHAPTER TEN

KENNEDY

"What did you want to know?" Ice set down his coffee and slipped into the stool next to me.

When I glanced over at him questioningly, he added, "Mannix said you might want me to explain my special brand of fucked up." He didn't look worried about referring to himself that way.

I cleared my throat and swallowed my mouthful of toast. "I was curious why you studied forensic pathology. I thought you'd do autopsies, and stuff like that."

"What makes you think I don't?" The smile he offered me was somehow sweet and sinister at the same time.

"Do you?" I nibbled on the corner of toast while he watched my mouth.

"Sometimes," he said lightly. "At uni I did. If I got a job with the local morgue, I might." He looked thoughtful as he sipped his coffee.

"And if you don't? What else are you going to do with a degree like that?" I remembered him shoving the knife into Eric Parcell's eyeball and suppressed a shiver. I bet they didn't teach that at university.

"I can show you if you want?" he offered. He chuckled at the suspicious look I gave him. "I wasn't suggesting I practice on you. I was just gonna show you my workroom. You might find it interesting and... Educational."

I had the distinct impression I'd find it disturbing as hell. At the same time, I was curious. Yeah, I knew what curiosity did to the cat, but I remembered his promise not to hurt me.

"Okay," I said finally. I hoped like hell I didn't regret agreeing to go.

"Do you trust me?" He cocked his head at me. He reminded me of a dog. Adorable when they lie on their back and let you rub their tummy, but if they wanted to tear you apart, they would. I'd only ever seen the tummy side of Ice. Unless you counted that night.

Now I knew the context, I was a lot less scared, but it was still disturbing as fuck.

My tongue flicked over my lips and gathered a few stray crumbs. I drew them in and swallowed them.

"I... I want to," I said slowly.

"But?" he prompted.

"But I hardly know you," I admitted. "Everything I learned yesterday really brought that home. It's one thing to care about someone and another to learn their whole life is—" I stopped to compose my thoughts. "Not what you thought it was."

"It's not everyday you learn your boyfriends are involved with organised crime." It was a statement, not a question.

"Exactly," I agreed.

"You understand why we didn't tell you straight away?" He looked anxious now. Worried I harboured resentment toward the guys for keeping something so important from me.

Did I?

"I do understand, but is there anything else I should know?" If they had any more enormous truth bombs, I wanted to know about them now. I'd had enough surprises to last for a long time. Unless they were pleasant ones, then I'd just as soon skip them.

"Yeah, that's why I want to show you my workroom." He downed the last of his coffee and hopped up off the stool. "If you can handle what you see there, then you can handle anything."

"I'm starting to think I should run away right now." But when he offered his hand, I accepted it.

"You'll be fine. I'm a better driver than Mannix. If you can survive his driving, then everything else after that should be easy."

"Those sound like famous last words if I ever heard them," I said.

He grinned. "Ares always says I should work in a funeral home, because I drive like I'm driving a hearse. Does that make you feel any better?"

"A little bit," I said. "As long as you don't expect me to ride in the back."

"The only way you'll be in the back is if I'm there too." He smiled suggestively.

I glanced back as we walked towards the garage. "Are the other guys coming too?"

"No, they left half an hour ago to go and do some stuff." He pressed the button on his fob and the garage door slowly slid open.

"Illegal stuff?" I couldn't resist asking.

He grinned. "Probably. They'll fill you in on all the details later."

"Are you sure about that?" I slipped into the passenger seat of his white, classic Corvette. Telling me about their lifestyle and giving me blow by blow descriptions were different things. Neither of them seemed inclined to share their shoe size, much less what they got up to when I wasn't around.

"Maybe not all the details," Ice conceded. "The important ones."

"Are those the ones they think I should know?" I clicked my seatbelt into place and sat back as he drove the Corvette out of the garage.

"Probably," he agreed. "But you know them. They're not the chatty type like me."

"It's probably best I don't know everything anyway," I said. "I'm still not sure what I think about all of this. Part of me is sure I should wait until you stop at a red light and jump out and run." How far would I get if I did? I suspected it wouldn't be far.

He glanced over and flashed me a smile. "If you're thinking of doing that, then I better not stop at any red lights. I hope there aren't any big trucks going through at the same time we are." He made a sound like squealing tires followed by a loud impact.

A beat later, he added, "I'm curious what it's like to be dead, but I don't want to find out today."

"Me either," I agreed. "Mostly I don't want to get out at a red light, so please stop when you get to one." That led me to ask, "Have you always been involved in, you know, illegal stuff? Were your parents involved in it too?"

"No idea about my father," he said lightly. "I was raised by my mother. He took off when I was a baby. I never knew him, or much about him. Just who he was. For all I know, you and I could be half brother and sister."

He glanced over and grinned.

I grimaced back at him. "Ewww, I hope not." Fucking my stepbrother was one thing. Doing it with an actual blood relative was something else entirely.

He chuckled at my reaction. "It wouldn't change anything between us for me. I'd still want to bury my cock as deep into your pussy as I can. But just to be sure, we can do a DNA test."

I didn't doubt him for a moment. If we discovered we were blood siblings, he'd still want to be with me. I should be grossed out, but for some reason I was slightly turned on.

Maybe we were related, because apparently I was fucked up in the head too.

"A DNA test might be a good idea," I said finally.

"Apparently my father was a serial cheater, and if my mother was connected to this place all along, then who knows what might have happened."

"I can take some samples at my workshop and send them off, but I'm sure they'll come back saying we're not related at all."

I wasn't sure if he was disappointed at the idea or pleased. Maybe a little of both. I didn't think it was because he actually wanted to screw his biological sister, but because he liked to push the envelope, and get away with things he shouldn't. Forbidden fruit and all that.

"While I'm there, I'll check Mannix and Ares too. How wild would it be if you were half sister to all three of us?" He chuckled to himself.

"I'm starting to see what Mannix means when he says you're fucked in the head," I said lightly. "Who thinks things like that?" Maybe I shouldn't *say* things like that, in case he was offended. He was driving after all.

He gave no sign of offence. Rather, he grinned. When he did that, he was too fucking cute for his own good, or mine. Or Mannix's, for that matter. The memory of him with his mouth around Mannix's cock, then my mouth around Ice's, made me hot all over.

For a little while there, I thought Ares was going to join in, but then he was getting himself off and Mannix was thrusting hard into me. It wasn't that long ago I was a virgin and now I'd been with two guys at once, while another watched.

I would never have dreamt it was possible, but I was one hundred percent here for every second of it.

"Just the Iceman," he said unapologetically. "I have a vivid imagination and a twisted sense of humour. I don't regret either of them."

"I'm sure you don't," I said. "There's nothing wrong with that. I have a pretty twisted sense of humour myself. As for my imagination, you don't want to know."

"I absolutely want to know, but we're here, so it may have to wait for a little while."

He pulled up the Corvette in front of a nondescript building. It looked like a derelict warehouse, but none of the windows were broken.

I climbed out of the low-slung car and looked more closely.

No, they weren't just broken, they were boarded up from the inside. Like whatever went on wasn't meant to be seen by the casual passerby.

The state-of-the-art keypad beside the door was at odds with the rest of the building. It looked relatively new. Dirty, like someone smeared soil or grease over it to make it look older, but free of rust, dents or worn out numbers.

Ice tapped in the combination and turned the knob to open the door.

"Let me say before we go in there that you can leave at any time. The combination is seven-five-nine-two. That will get you in or out. Obviously, don't share that with anyone."

He waved me inside and closed the door behind me.

I ran the combination over in my head a few times so I wouldn't forget. I doubted he shared the combination with anyone but Mannix and Ares. And now me. If he was trying to earn my trust, he was doing a good job of it.

Assuming he was telling the truth about the code letting me back out. And that it was the right code in the first place.

I found myself in a virtually empty room that looked as worn as the outside of the building. Only a table and a few chairs sat against one wall. A few hooks hung on the opposite wall. Right now they were empty, but they looked like the kind you'd hang a jacket on. A single bulb hung from the ceiling.

"This is... Cosy," I said. It looked like the kind of place you'd see on TV, where the bad guy took the innocent victim to be horribly murdered. I swallowed hard and repeated the code over and over again in my head.

"This is just the reception area. In case anyone does break in, we make it look as harmless as possible." He walked over to a doorway at the end of the room and pushed down the handle.

Instead of the door opening, a hatch in the floor slid back.

"Lucky I wasn't standing right there." I stared at the sudden hole with wide eyes.

"I wouldn't have let you stand *right there,*" he said. "I save that for my enemies."

I couldn't tell from the expression on his face whether he was joking or not, so I decided he wasn't. Although, since the hole led to a set of stairs, I decided his enemies wouldn't get too badly hurt from the drop anyway.

I decided not to think too hard about him having enemies in the first place. I guessed that came with the territory of being a mobster.

"Your workshop is down there?" I peered into the darkness.

"Cool, isn't it?" he asked. "No one knows it's here but us and the occasional special guest."

Special guest? Did he actually mean—

He started down the stairs. Not wanting to be left behind in the dingy space, I quickly followed.

CHAPTER ELEVEN

KENNEDY

The first thing I noticed when we reached the bottom was the tang of what smelled like blood.

Yeah, it probably was blood.

I stepped into what looked like a horror movie.

Or a nightmare.

A couple of large hooks were bolted to the ceiling. The chains that hung from them were stained with something dark. The concrete floor underneath was similarly stained.

A long, wooden work table like the ones we had in art class at school sat a couple of metres from the chains. At the moment, there was nothing on it. Nothing but the same stains as the rest of the room. And other stains, it looked like someone tried to bleach the surface of the wood. Long scratches and gouges were embedded in the timber.

To the side of the room, a metal chair was bolted to the floor. Restraints were attached to the arms and legs, reminiscent of Charlie's couch, but a lot less comfortable.

Beside that, was a small table, pliers and scalpels laid out in a menacing display. Ready for... Whatever Ice would use them for.

"What is this place?" I asked. I turned around slowly, taking in the exposed, grey brick walls and the dim light. We were underground, so there were no windows. It was the kind of place someone came to die a horrible death.

"It's just my workroom," he said like it was no big deal. "Sometimes we find people who don't want to be forthcoming with information that we need. It's my job to get them to share."

I stopped to look at him.

"You torture people for information?" Of course he did, what else would go on in a place like this?

"I prefer to think of it as persuasion, but yes," he agreed. "I extensively studied human anatomy so I knew exactly where to work on people. Where it hurts the most and how to keep them alive. It's a last resort, but sometimes a necessary one."

My heart thundered in my chest. "How many people have you..."

"Enough," he said vaguely. "I'll spare you the specifics." He stepped over to me and slipped his arms around me. "You haven't run away yet."

I was resistant to embracing him for a few moments. "Will I end up restrained to that chair if I do?"

He looked over to it and chuckled. "Not unless you want me to. If it'll make you feel better, I'll let you restrain me."

Before I could answer or melt against him, voices and the sound of scuffling came from the top of the stairs.

"Things might just get interesting. " Ice tipped his head back and looked up to the upper level.

Mannix and Ares carried someone between them. A man, judging by the height and physique.

When they reached the bottom of the stairs, I saw the man's mouth was duct taped shut. His eyes were wide with fear and defiance.

He kicked out, but they dragged him over to the chains. All three guys attached them to him. Manacles snapped around his wrists, forcing him to hold them up over his head.

"Well, well, what do we have here?" Ice stood

back and crossed his arms over his chest. He looked appraisingly at the struggling man.

"We did a bit of digging into this asshole," Mannix said. He turned to me. "You recognise him?"

I frowned. "Now you mention it, he's the father of one of my newer students. What is he doing down here?" I'd only seen him once or twice, but he gave me the creeps both times. What was his name?

Nixon.

Frank Nixon.

"The cameras caught him getting into his car the night you were followed," Ares said, his eyes firmly on Nixon. "The same kind of car that followed you."

"That doesn't necessarily mean anything," I pointed out.

Nixon nodded vigourously. He made an incoherent sound of agreement through the tape.

"It might not," Mannix agreed. "Except he works for the Bell family, as an enforcer. He and his family have only been in Dusk Bay for a couple of months. The same amount of time we've been having trouble with people like him. I want to know why he followed you. Unfortunately, Mr Nixon here hasn't been forthcoming with any information."

Ice was wearing a sleeveless T-shirt, muscular biceps on display, but he pretended to roll up his sleeves. At the same time, he smiled. The whole look was adorably sinister.

"Perfect. Anyone who comes after my Beautiful gets special treatment."

Nixon struggled harder and tried to speak. Or maybe to scream.

Mannix curled his hand into my hair. "You don't have to be here for this, Princess. One of us can take you home."

A normal person would take him up on his offer, but I realised by now that I wasn't as normal as I thought I was. If anything, I was intrigued. The man followed me. Who knows what he would have done if he caught up with me?

What had Ice said about Mannix's brother Gunnar? He beat the crap out of people to keep them in line. Would Nixon have done that to me?

"I want to stay," I said finally.

"That's our girl," Ice said approvingly. He grabbed hold of a corner of the piece of duct tape and yanked it off in one go.

I winced. That had to hurt.

Nixon groaned and swore. "You assholes have the wrong guy. I work in a bottle-shop. I've never followed anyone home in my life."

"Then why do you have regular payments from Samuel Bell in your bank account?" Mannix asked.

"I've never heard of him," Nixon said, but he was clearly rattled. He knew he was fucked.

Not in a good way.

Ice looked over to his small table and picked up the pliers.

"You want to try again?" He did nothing with them, he just stood tapping them against his opposite hand. It was enough to make Nixon scared, and send a jolt of heat right to my core.

Holy fucked up shit, Iceman.

Nixon looked around at us frantically. His eyes locked on me as though he thought I'd be his way out.

"Why did you follow me?" I asked coldly. I was surprised by the calm steel in my own voice. The lack of a waiver; of hesitation.

You don't choose the thug life, I thought.

Nixon said nothing.

Ice grabbed one of his hands and clamped the pliers onto his ring finger. He squeezed tight.

Nixon's eyes widened. He was obviously in a shit load of pain, but he didn't make a sound.

"High pain threshold," Ice said, "my favourite." He squeezed harder.

Nixon's finger crunched as his bone was broken. Now he cried out.

I really shouldn't have been turned on, but I was.

"Our Princess is enjoying this," Mannix said. "Let's make the most of it."

"Another finger it is." Ice pressed the pliers down onto another of Nixon's fingers, squeezing so hard the bone must have shattered. Both fingers were a bloodied mess.

Nixon gritted his teeth and grunted through the pain. "I was only doing my job."

"Now we're getting somewhere." Ice applied the pliers to a third finger. "What exactly was your job?"

Nixon groaned. "I was supposed to send a message to your family."

"Ever tried texting?" Ice asked.

Nixon responded with a humourless snort.

"What was the message?" Mannix tightened his grip on my hair.

"The message was that you're vulnerable," Nixon said. "They wanted me to take out Leo's step-daughter to show they could get to you."

I blinked. "Your job was to kill me?"

"Scare you, then wait until after they tightened security, and then kill you. They wanted Leo to know it didn't matter what he did, they could get to him and anyone affiliated with the Brantleys."

"Why me?" That should have scared me, and it did, really, but mostly it pissed me off.

"They probably thought you were an easy target," Ares said. "They misjudged. They sent someone who lacks the skills to carry out something like that."

"Right. If they wanted to take out Kennedy, they needed to send an assassin," Ice said. "Not a third rate thug." He squeezed the pliers down on Nixon's thumb.

Nixon howled in pain.

I couldn't bring myself to conjure up even a little bit of sympathy for him. He would have killed me and not given it a second thought. I didn't want to spare too much thought for what he might have done to me *before* he killed me.

If his boss wanted to send a message, it might include, 'P.S. We can toy with Leo's people as much as we want.'

"How would you have killed me?" I didn't know why it mattered, but it did. Some part of me needed, wanted, to know what I was up against. If nothing else, it served to further justify the guy's killing Eric Parcell. If this was the war they claimed it was, what or who else might come at me?

"Answer the woman." Ice moved the pliers to Nixon's pinky finger, but didn't squeeze yet. It was the only finger on his hand that wasn't shattered and covered in blood. If he got out of here alive, he wouldn't be using his hand again.

Yeah, boo fucking hoo.

"The boss wanted it done in a personal way." Nixon's voice was weaker now as the pain closed in harder on him. "He wanted you to know he could get to any of you as much as he wanted to."

"That's fucked up," I remarked. "You would have, what? Strangled me?" The thought of his hands around my throat robbed me of air for a few moments.

He gasped out the word, "Yeah."

Ice nodded towards the pliers. "Do you want a turn?"

"It's okay if you do." Mannix turned my face and pressed his lips to mine. "He would have wrapped his fingers around your neck and squeezed. He would have watched while you struggled for air. He would have held you down while you fought back. He would have watched the light leave your eyes and felt your body become lifeless. People like him, they enjoy every minute of it. Don't think you would have been his first. Or his last."

His words set my blood on fire.

"Have you killed women before?" I needed the answer to that, even knowing how horrifying it might be. My stomach twisted, rebelled.

"Yeah," Nixon said. "When the boss wanted me to." Any hint of his former denial was gone, replaced by a sickening sense of pride in the horrible things he'd done.

I stepped towards him.

He tried to step back, but the chains held him in place.

"Did you enjoy it?" I locked my gaze on his, unflinching, even as a small part of me protested my being here in doing this.

Shut up, I told it. *This is your life now. You can't unknow or unsee anything. You might as well enjoy it.*

The power of standing in front of someone twice my size, knowing he couldn't fight back, knowing he deserved what was coming to him, was heady as fuck. Mannix was right. This was addictive. No one but us would ever know exactly what went on here today. Not the police, no one.

The smile Nixon gave me was chilling and vicious. "Yeah, I enjoyed it. I would have enjoyed strangling you. I bet you would have put up a fight, but you wouldn't have won. Your life would have been mine to end."

Yeah, he wasn't unhinged at all, was he? I saw it in his eyes that he was imagining what it would be like to hold me down with the weight of his body and watch my life end. He would have gotten off on killing me. The experience would have been orgasmic for him.

That same small part of me I just told to shut up, reminded me I was getting off on this too. That it made me almost as bad as him.

Not as bad, I reasoned, because I did nothing to warrant his boss sending him after me. I did nothing but be Leo's stepdaughter. As far as I knew, that wasn't a crime anywhere in the world.

I reached my hand out for the pliers.

Without a word, Ice lay them across my palm. They felt warm from his touch, slick with Nixon's blood.

I gripped the handle and held Nixon's pinky finger with the end of the pliers before I squeezed.

"This is for the women you killed. You won't be killing any more of us." Flesh and bone gave way under the pressure, like squashing a chicken bone. The crack and crunch, and his howl of pain were the most satisfying sounds I've heard apart from the guys' grunts when they came.

"Do you want to start on his other hand?" Ice offered.

I shook my head. "No." I handed him the pliers before I turned and trotted up the stairs. I managed to key in the passcode and step outside into the fresh air before I threw up every bit of my breakfast.

CHAPTER TWELVE

Mannix found me a couple of minutes later, sitting on the sidewalk with my back against the building. I'd pulled my knees up to my chest and wrapped my arms around my legs.

"You shouldn't be out here by yourself." He sat down beside me and placed his arm over my shoulders.

"I'm not by myself," I said faintly. "You're here too."

He chuckled. "I am now, but fuck knows what might have happened before I got here."

This part of town was all but deserted, which made it perfect for Ice's workroom, and for me to sit outside for two or three minutes by myself.

I understood the reason for his warning and concern. Of course I did. I wasn't going to quickly forget what I heard inside. And what I did. I swallowed hard.

"It's always confronting the first time," he said. "I threw my guts up too, but I did it in front of everyone. It wasn't my finest hour. You become used to it after a while." He nuzzled his face into my hair. "You don't have to come back here again if you don't want to."

I shook my head slightly. "That's not it. I should have found that... disgusting, or terrifying, or something." It was all of those things, but it was more than that.

"You're surprised by how much you enjoyed it?" he guessed. "You're worried about what it says about you and what we'll think."

"Is it sick to enjoy getting revenge for those women?" I asked. "Is it even sicker that I'm not sure it was about getting revenge? I think maybe I did it because I wanted to. What does that make me?"

He kissed my temple. "It makes you one of us. Neither Ares nor I get as much of a kick out of it as Ice, so we leave him to it, but we could do all that shit too if we wanted to. If you hadn't broken his pinky finger, I would have. No one goes after my princess and gets away with it. But you know what, when we let him go, he'll go crawling back to his boss with a message from us. Don't fuck with our girl."

"What if he sends someone else?" I asked. "Like an actual assassin." From what I knew about them, I wouldn't see them coming. I'd be dead and that was it.

No thanks.

"If he does, we'll deal with it." Mannix's tone was firm, confident, reassuring. "But I don't think Samuel Bell will send an assassin after you. He'd send one after Dad. If you're going to spend that much on a hit, you go after the big dog. If not Dad, then he'd go after Daisy Lasalle, or one of her boyfriends. Or maybe even Caleb or Reuben Brantley themselves, if he's feeling like he's got bigger balls than usual."

I wasn't sure if I should be relieved or offended that I wasn't important enough to send an assassin to kill me. Maybe a bit of both. But a whole lot of the first one.

I put that aside for now. "So you don't think I'm sick for what I did?"

"Not even a little bit," he assured me. "And none of us will think you're sick if you want to go in there and pull off some of Nixon's toenails. Or cut off his balls with Ice's scalpel. Or whatever you and Ice come up with to teach him not to come after you."

None of that should have made me hot, but it all did. Every last word.

"Last night when we were dancing, you mentioned punishment for running away," I said slowly. "You didn't mean this, did you?" I jerked my head toward the building behind us.

"I meant spanking, but if you want to take it further than that, I'm game." He grinned.

"What do you have in mind?" I asked carefully.

He stood and pulled me to my feet. "Do you trust me?"

That was the second time today one of the guys asked me that and I answered him the way I answered Ice.

"I trust you."

"Excellent. Just remember, if you want to stop, you only have to say so."

Now I was somewhere between nervous and excited. Both of those built when he led me back into the building and down the stairs.

Nixon was still hanging by his wrists. Blood trickled down one arm.

Ares was leaning against the wall, arms crossed over his chest, eyes half closed. He actually managed to look bored.

Ice stood over at the sink, washing blood off the pliers.

"You're just in time for round two. I was about to start decorating him with my scalpel, for shits and giggles. And in case he has more information he'd like to share." He put the pliers aside on the edge of the sink and grabbed up the scalpel.

"I thought we might have some fun at the same time," Mannix said. He gave me a look to remind me I could opt out at any time, but took me over to the set of chains that hung parallel to the ones around Nixon's wrists.

I eyed him doubtfully for a moment, but let him fasten the ends of the chain to my wrists. I was maybe a metre away from Nixon but while he looked defeated I felt elated. And curious. And a little terrified.

Mannix nodded to Ice.

Ice raised the scalpel and sliced it down the side of Nixon's cheek.

"I know you're wondering how I came to have such neat work," Ice said to the man, "it's from years of practice. When I first started out, my cuts were much messier than this."

"He's not joking." Mannix walked over to a set of drawers beside the sink and pulled out another scalpel. "His cuts looked more like chew marks."

Ares snorted a laugh.

Ice pretended to look offended. "They weren't *that* bad."

"Says you." Mannix stepped back over to me and held the scalpel a centimetre from my throat.

I held my breath and struggled to keep from swallowing or freaking out.

"That's my brave girl." He moved the scalpel down slowly, slicing the fabric of my T-shirt as he went.

"Wait a sec," Ice said. "If our girl is going to be naked, he doesn't get to look."

He went over to the same draw Mannix got the scalpel and pulled out what looked like a thick nail and a small mallet.

Nixon started to struggle against his chains. "Nonononono! I'll keep my eyes closed. I swear! Fuck... No!"

Ice placed the nail in front of his eyeball and tapped it with the mallet. Once. Twice.

"Don't want to kill the guy."

Nixon screamed.

And again when Ice took out his other eye.

Ice set the implements aside. "There we go. You can all be as naked as you want to."

Mannix nodded his thanks and went back to slicing through my clothes, until they all lay on the floor at my feet.

My nipples pebbled harder than rocks when Ice made a neat incision in Nixon's other cheek. Blood poured down Nixon's face and trickled onto his shirt. Stains spread where it landed.

Mannix put the scalpel down and parted my thighs with his hands. He slipped his fingers between my legs, brought them up to my pussy. His eyes widened.

"Princess, you're drenched. You really do get off on this." He started to trace light circles around my clit with one hand and around one nipple with the other. "Keep your eyes on Nixon. Watch what Ice is doing to him. Enjoy it."

I *was* enjoying it. The sight of all that blood and pain, and the feel of Mannix's touch.

Ice stopped his slicing for a moment to lean over and lick and suck my other nipple. "Mmmm, you taste extra delicious today." He smiled adorably at me. How could he be so cute and yet so bloodthirsty at the same time?

Mannix knelt on the stained floor, parted my legs wider and dove in between my thighs with his lips and tongue.

He muttered something that sounded like, "Definitely delicious."

To my surprise, Ares stepped over to me. He moved around behind me, put his arms around me and started to knead my breasts. He wasn't gentle, but his touch was pure electricity. Like he was finally giving in to the attraction between us, and it pissed him off, but he was going to throw all of himself into it anyway.

I leaned back into him, so my back was pressed against his chest. With my hands chained above my head, I couldn't touch him the way I wanted to, but that only turned me on harder. The guys had all the control. All I could do was enjoy it.

I groaned as Mannix slipped a couple of fingers inside me. He started to fuck me with his hand and his tongue.

At the same time, Ares' fingers became bruising on my delicate skin.

"I'm going to leave my mark on you, Firecracker," he said in my ear. "Lots of them."

Fuck, yes, please.

He moved around to the side of me and leaned over my breast. He traced patterns over my skin with his tongue, then gripped it hard between his teeth and bit me.

I let out the little whimper I knew he liked so much. If he was trying to keep his cock out of my pussy, he wasn't trying very hard.

He bit me again in another spot, hard enough to draw blood. "All the marks."

I cried out in a combination of pleasure and pain, overwhelmed by all of my senses. At some point, the smell of blood became the scent of sex. I couldn't differentiate between the two.

Letting the chain bear my weight, I rocked against Mannix's mouth. I was so turned on right now I must be dribbling down my own thighs.

I came suddenly, hard and fast, my scream mingling with Nixon's as Ice cut off a good chunk of his left ear. Not so much that he couldn't hear, but it would have hurt like a bitch.

I'd barely come down when Mannix leaned me back against Ares's chest. He undid the front of his jeans and pushed them down far enough to free his erection. He placed his hands behind my knees and lifted my legs up to his waist. With a grunt, he pulled me onto his cock.

I moaned. I may never get enough of being filled by one of their cocks. It was like pure, thick bliss.

Somewhere in the back of my mind, I was aware of Ares also undoing and pushing down his jeans. He fitted his cock into the crease of my ass and thrust against me at the same time Mannix thrust into me.

"It's a shame you're missing this, Nixon," Ice said conversationally. "It's really hot. I know, I know, you can't see. I'm sure you can imagine it. But don't imagine it, because I might need to stab your brain if you're thinking about our girlfriend like that."

Nixon grunted something unintelligible. It was likely all he was thinking about was his pain, and wishing Ice would hurry up and kill him.

"The more I get to know you, the more perfect you are," Mannix told me. "So perfect."

It figured that most girls wouldn't get turned on or want to be fucked while someone was chained up beside her been tortured. Right now, I didn't care if it was wrong. It felt right. Good.

Mannix thrust harder and faster, his sweated skin sliding on mine.

Ares ground into me, rubbing himself and grunting near my ear. At the same time, his hands gripped my breasts so tight it brought tears to my eyes. I didn't want him to stop.

Both guys came nearly in unison, a beat after I came for a second time. Our cries eventually dwindled down to silence.

"What a shame," Ice said with a sigh. "He passed out."

CHAPTER THIRTEEN

ICE

I pushed open the door to Kennedy's room without knocking. It was already ajar, so I figured she wouldn't mind. Besides, I was kinda hoping to catch her off guard, or asleep. I would have woken her up.

I found her lying on her bed on her stomach, her laptop open in front of her. Her mesmerising eyes were focused on the screen. The colours in front of her lit her face. They made her look ethereal, like the goddess she was.

I lay down beside her and looked at her laptop.

"Studying again, I see." I overlapped my hands in front of me and rested my chin on them.

"Unless you've got some method to deliver information into my brain without me reading it, and then outputting it just from my thoughts, then yeah." She glanced over at me and smiled ruefully.

"I'll get on that." I grinned back at her. "But I warn you, it might not be ready until after you finish your degree."

"Figures." She closed the laptop and rolled over onto her back. Her eyes toward the ceiling, she let out a soft breath. "What happened the other day, in your workroom..."

"I'm an open book about all of it. Anything you want to ask me, go ahead and ask." I long ago got past any reservations I had about the things I did. I wasn't going to apologise for a drop of blood spilt, or scream of pain I drew from the people I worked with.

"You've done it a lot?"

"You could say that," I agreed. "I haven't lost count, but you probably don't want to know the particulars." It was like sexual partners. It was enough to know whether or not someone had experience. The exact details didn't matter. Not to me anyway.

She looked over at me now. "Does it ever make you feel, I don't know, grossed out?"

I answered her question with one of my own. "Regrets? It's easy to get caught up in the moment and then later on wish you hadn't."

"Not regrets exactly," she said. Her brow creased adorably. "I feel like I should have regrets or be sickened. Or something. But then I think about what he would have done to me and I don't feel bad about it at all. I feel—"

"Vindicated? Turned on?" I guessed.

She let out a grunt so soft I almost missed hearing it.

"A bit of those too. Mostly I feel... I don't know if powerful is the right word. I mean, we could have done anything to him and no one could stop us. It's so wrong, but at the same time..."

"Fucking awesome," I finished for her. "I started because I was fascinated with how bodies worked, but inflicting pain on people who have, or would, inflict it on other people is a rush. I was pissed that I didn't get to do that with Eric Parcell. Mannix was in a hurry. Our friend, Mr Nixon, made up for it."

"Is he..." she asked tentatively.

"Dead? No. Not yet." He wished he was. He'd begged me to kill him, but for what he would have done to Kennedy, he was getting what he deserved. It would have been a lot worse for him if he'd actually touched her. I could work slower and a lot more painfully if I needed to. Only three people got to touch her: me, Mannix and Ares. I didn't even want her touching herself. There was no need for her to get herself off when we could do that for her.

I rolled onto my side. "Do you want me to kill him? Because I can do that if that's what you want." I would do anything, or kill almost anyone, for her. If she wanted me to kill Mannix or Ares, I'd have to think twice about that. They were my brothers and they accepted me when the rest of the world didn't, or wouldn't. I'd do or kill anything or anyone for them too.

Her throat bobbed up and down as she swallowed. "Do you think he's suffered enough? I know what he would have done, but he didn't get to do it."

I kissed the tip of her nose. "You're so adorably big-hearted. If it means that much to you, I'll put him out of his misery in the morning." He was starting to get smelly and was making my workroom messy anyway.

"Thank you," she said softly. She looked like she wanted to ask something, but wasn't sure if she should.

"You want to come and watch?" I offered.

"Is it wrong that I do?" she asked.

"First of all, no, it's not wrong at all," I said firmly. "Second of all, you don't need validation from anyone but yourself. If the idea of pain, blood and death turns you on, that's completely okay. It gives me a raging hard-on every time. Are we normal? Maybe not. Do I give a fuck? Not even a small one. And neither should you. I'll bet you a million dollars Mannix told you the same thing."

"Yeah, he did, I just—" She exhaled softly out her nose. "Being told it's okay and accepting it myself are different things. You know?"

"I do know," I said. "I've been through all of the same feelings you're going through now. We all have. But you know the other guys got off as much as you did. We're all a twisted, dysfunctional, fucked up family. Which, in my opinion, is the best kind."

She was silent for a moment. When she spoke again it was to ask, "Has my mother been to your workroom?"

I pretended to misunderstand the meaning of her question. "Do you think she should?"

Kennedy batted me on the arm. "No, I don't. I just thought if she knew about all the things then maybe she'd gone there and saw the things you do."

"Your mother has yet to grace my workroom with her presence," I said grandly. "In case you're curious, Leo has, but only once or twice. He's generally the kind of guy who orders a thing to be done and expects it to get done, but doesn't necessarily want to know or see the details. The only time he drops by is to see if we're spending his money the way he expects us to. He gets pissy about waste."

That was unfortunate. I'd be more than happy to have him sit in on the fun and games more often.

On the other hand, Mannix preferred his father to leave things like that to him. It helped to grow his influence in the business, and his ego. It wouldn't hurt Mannix when he took over his father's business if he had influence his father didn't.

If it was me, I'd have my eyes on every aspect, no matter how messy. That way, it was easier to discern if someone was trying to screw you over. We wouldn't, but Leo couldn't know that if he stayed away.

Telling him how to run his business was the top of a long list of things I would never do. I kept my nose out of it and did what was asked of me.

"Does this Samuel Bell have people who do for him what you do for Leo?" she asked.

"Without doubt," I said. "I've heard his stepson, Zachary, has a taste for blood. And possibly for his stepsister Chloe. From what I've heard, she and her twin sister, Lila are as nasty as two people can be. Before I met you, I would have happily been the meat in a Bell sister sandwich."

"What does it say about me if you have a thing for nasty people?" She raised her eyebrows at me.

"Either it says you're nastier than you think you are, or it says I'm reformed," I replied. "I'll leave that for you to decide." I kissed her forehead.

"I'm guessing it's the first one." Her freckled brow wrinkled cutely. "Not more than five minutes ago, I asked to come along and see a man die."

"Unfortunately, nastiness is wildly underrated as a positive character trait." I curled a section of her hair around my fingers. "The best people in the world are the nastiest. I can think of four straight off the top of my head."

She responded by speaking slowly. "You, Mannix, my mother, and Leo?"

I laughed. "You, Mannix, Ares and me," I corrected. "No offence to your mother or Leo, but I don't think either of them could be called nasty. Not the way the rest of us are."

"I didn't realise there was a measurement scale for something like that." She rolled back onto her stomach and lay on her arms. Her breasts were pushed forward enticingly.

"Sweet girl, there's a measurement scale for everything. It doesn't matter what it is, someone will rate it. People love to organise and quantify everything."

"Is that your professional observation, Doctor Miller?" she teased.

"Definitely." I liked the way that sounded, coming from her lips. I was a long way off being able to call myself that, but if she kept saying that, I might just be driven to keep on studying.

"Are you planning to do a PhD too?" I ask her. "Doctor Knight has a ring to it."

She snorted softly. "I'd sound like a supervillain. If I did that, I have to get myself a cat."

I grinned. "We could all be doctors except Mannix. Although, knowing him, if we all went and did our PhDs, he'd feel left out if he didn't do it too."

"Or he could just buy himself one." Her expression was wry.

I snapped my fingers. "Or you could hack into whichever university you like and give us all PhDs."

I frowned and quickly corrected myself. "Don't hack into Brutham Academy. Doing that would shorten your life expectancy by a large amount."

"Is it really that bad?" She didn't look as alarmed as I might have expected. If anything, she looked curious. Hopefully not too curious to try it, because I wasn't exaggerating. Brutham Academy was as possessive of its digital data as me and the other guys were of Kennedy.

"At the end of first year, they let third and fourth years hunt us down," I said. "If we've made the right alliances and haven't pissed off the wrong people, we might just survive. Obviously, the three of us did."

Her eyes widened. "Wait a minute. By hunt you down you mean—"

"Exactly that. We're given a starting position and a location we need to get to. If we get there without anyone catching up with us, we pass. If we didn't, I wouldn't be here telling you this."

Her lips dropped apart. "They're literally allowed to kill students if they catch up with them?"

"They're not just allowed to, they're *encouraged* to. This life is tough. Only the strongest, best connected and smartest, survive. On the upside, we got to do the same to the first years when it was our turn. It was... exhilarating. But we weren't killing for the fun of it. The first years who weren't connected, and allied with other powerful students, were often ones who were ostracised for a reason."

"They touched the wrong guy's girlfriend?" Kennedy guessed.

"That's certainly been a reason for someone to be targeted in the past." And would be a reason for it in the future. Most of the guys in this life were brought up to understand that they protect their woman at all costs. I couldn't think of a single one who wasn't the, 'touch her and you die,' type.

"I'm starting to think the world is a different place than what I thought it was." She sighed.

"In a good way, or in a bad way?" I tangled my fingers tighter in her hair.

"I don't know yet. Maybe a bit of both." She looked thoughtful for a moment. "How reliant is Samuel Bell on his computer systems?"

I smiled. "Very. Do you have something in mind?"

CHAPTER FOURTEEN

I'd needed to have this conversation for ages, but now the moment was here, I didn't know how to start it.

"Coffee?" I asked as I added water to the coffee machine. If in doubt, lead with caffeine.

"I'll never say no to coffee." Mum slipped into a stool and rested her elbows on the marble counter-top. Her engagement and wedding rings were so chunky and ornate, they took up most of her finger between her knuckle and the first joint. Any bigger and she wouldn't have been able to bend the digit.

"So... Nice honeymoon?" We might as well continue with small talk.

"It was lovely." She smiled like a woman head over heels in love. It was adorable in an, 'ewww, mushy stuff with my parent,' kind of way.

"New Zealand is beautiful at this time of year. Any time of year really. We went on a helicopter ride in Rotorua and landed on the side of Mount Tarawera. The view was incredible. And the dormant volcano wasn't bad either." She gave me an exaggerated wink.

My mother's attempt at winking left a lot to be desired at the best of times.

"I thought about asking the pilot to fly us back home so he could meet you, but you seem somewhat busy right now." She didn't even try to hide the fact she was fishing. She clearly wanted an update on me and the guys.

I might give her one, once she was forthcoming with what I wanted to know.

"Did you know Leo was involved in organ-ised crime?" Shit, I hadn't intended to be that blunt, but when the words were out, they were out.

The coffee machine bubbled and started to pour out an espresso.

Such an ordinary sound as the counterpoint to an extraordinary question.

She didn't flinch. She didn't even blink. Not even one drop of surprise showed on her face.

"Yes," she said simply. "I've known since before I

met him. How do you think we were able to afford the lifestyle we had before Leo?"

Yeah, I suspected that, but to hear the words coming from her mouth was a different thing altogether. Especially with no attempt to deny anything. I thought she'd at least hesitate.

She placed a palm on the countertop and leaned over closer.

"Before you get all worked up, I didn't tell you because you didn't need to know at the time. I wanted to keep you out of that life for as long as possible."

I stepped back until I was pressed against the bench in front of the coffee maker, physically as far as I could get while being in the same kitchen.

"Not forever?" I asked. "Why would you want me involved in it at all?"

She raised her hand briefly to gesture around the kitchen. "Because most people can't afford places like this. I want the best for you. I want you to have everything you need and want, without having to worry about where the next meal is coming from. If that means stepping into morally grey territory, so be it."

"So you made that choice for me when you asked

me to come to Dusk Bay?" I asked. "You knew what would happen?"

"Not really." She sat back. "The most I expected was that you would finish your degree and leave to get on with your life. I didn't realise you'd let those boys drag you in so deep or so quick." That was definitely a look of disapproval on her face.

It was a bit fucking late for that.

"Why does that bother you?" I handed her the coffee, then put my cup in place in the coffee machine to let it fill.

"Because there's morally grey, and then there's those three boys." She curled her hands around her cup. "Mannix seems very ambitious. I'm not sure Isaac is all there, and Ares is downright grumpy and unpleasant."

I couldn't help my body from stiffening the way it did when she spoke.

None of what she said was wrong, not exactly, but there was so much more to them than that.

"I like them," I said, my voice tight. "Leo doesn't seem to mind Mannix and I being together." If there was anyone's opinion Mum cared about, it was Leo's.

"Leo might be slightly shortsighted where his son is concerned." She sipped her coffee. "Maybe I should talk to him."

Maybe I should fling my hot coffee in her face and see how it sounded when she screamed.

Where the fuck did that thought come from? I should try to get some more sleep. Clearly I wasn't getting enough right now.

The coffee machine finished and I picked up my cup, but held onto it carefully. Just in case it jumped out of my hands and threw itself at her.

"There's no need for that." I tried to keep my voice light, but this whole conversation had me on edge. "I'm an adult and I can make my own choices. You wanted me to come here and get involved with this lifestyle. You don't get to choose how that happens."

Her expression changed to one I'd never seen before. Dangerous, a clear warning.

"If Leo orders Mannix to stay away from you, Mannix will have no choice but to obey him. Same with the other two. If that happens, it will only be because we have your best interests at heart. Those boys are trouble."

"Only because Leo tells them to be," I said coldly.

"Right up until Mannix's ambition gets too big for him to listen to his father anymore."

"Is that what this is about?" I asked. "Leo is

worried Mannix is going to step on his toes?" To hear Mannix talk, Leo might be justified in those concerns, but no time soon. "It seems to me like we all have bigger fish to fry. Like Samuel Bell."

Now she looked surprised. "How do you know about him?"

I snorted a bitter laugh and told her everything, except what happened in the workroom. No doubt she knew the details of what went on down there, but if she didn't, she wasn't going to hear it from me. Especially the bit about me using pliers on Frank Nixon. I suspected that was the kind of thing she meant when she said the guys were dragging me down into the dark.

Personally, I wondered if I was there all along, it just took time for my life to catch up with my proclivities.

"So it was Samuel Bell who had you followed?" She looked furious. "You didn't think to tell me this sooner?"

"You were busy getting married," I reminded her. "And then you were on your honeymoon. Besides, you seem to know more about all of this than I do. I'm surprised you didn't know already."

Had Mannix not told Leo? The last thing I

wanted to do was throw Mannix under the bus with his father. That would only create more tension, and right now there was enough of that going around.

"Besides, I know nothing about Samuel Bell except he seems to have taken a dislike to me."

Mum hopped off her stool and came around the island to me.

"I'll never let anything happen to you."

I was taller than her when she didn't wear heels, but she still had that fierce, tiger mother thing going on. I could almost imagine her with a set of pliers in her hand, ready to pull off the eyelids of anyone who dared to think about hurting her baby.

Almost.

I might be projecting, because that sounded like something I'd be tempted to do if anyone came after a child of mine. That included the students from the gym. Hurting children was the worst crime I could think of. Stealing their innocence, scarring their small bodies. Anyone who did that got exactly what they deserved.

She closed her eyes and rubbed the tip of her fingers across her forehead. Her fingernails were blood red, like she needed the camouflage if she ever scratched anyone's eyes out.

"I'm starting to think I should have let you stay in

Sydney. You were safer there." She sounded tired. Frustrated. Like all she wanted to do was keep me safe, but instead she'd dragged me straight into the lion's den. Dangerous though it might be, it was also secure.

"Was I? I'm still Leo's stepdaughter. This place is much more secure than uni ever was. I would have been a sitting duck up there." No one would have stopped Frank Nixon from getting to me on or around campus.

"There are other places," she said.

"Brutham Academy?" I suggested, half-joking. I doubted I would have made it to the end of first year. Or would I? My mother's relationship with Leo might have given me connections that saw me get past the trial Ice told me about. Added to that, I was fit, athletic and quick. I should give myself more credit for being a badass.

"That would be one good option," she agreed. "I went there. They would have updated the security several times since then."

I shook my head. What the fuck did she just say?

"You went there?" Just when I thought she couldn't surprise me anymore, she came out with that little gem. Had she killed anyone?

No, I did *not* want to know the answer to that.

Not in this lifetime or the next. Some secrets were better kept hidden.

I was starting to wonder who this woman standing in front of me really was. She looked like my mother, she sounded like her, but the things she said blew my mind.

I lightly touched her arm. "Just checking I'm not dreaming." I put my cup down and leaned over the counter on my elbows.

"I feel like I've entered some kind of alternate reality. Or an episode of a superhero TV show where they're all bad guys for that forty minutes. Only, this seems to be my life."

She laughed. "None of us are bad guys. Not exactly. We just like to get what we want and, unlike the average person, we've found a way to do it. Sometimes it's slightly illegal—"

I snorted a laugh. "Sometimes?" As far as I could tell, it was more than slightly illegal a lot of the time. Bad guys was both a relative and a subjective term.

She was right about one thing, there was an awful lot of grey involved in all of this. I couldn't remember the last time I saw the world in black and white, but things were more and more complicated and convoluted the longer I was here in Dusk Bay.

"Yes, only sometimes," she agreed. "Only when it's completely necessary. Otherwise, people like Leo are nothing more than savvy business people. He sees an opportunity and he grabs it. And he has enough money to make it happen. There's nothing wrong with that."

"That depends who gets stepped on along the way." My expression was wry. "I suspect a few people wouldn't agree with that assumption."

"Of course not. You can't please everyone. At the end of the day, the best thing you can do is please yourself and those you care about. No one else really matters."

"You sound like Leo," I remarked. "Actually, you sound like Mannix and Ice. They're passionately dedicated to taking care of people they care about. Including me and each other. Maybe if you got to know them—"

"I'd still know they're trouble," she interrupted. "It's easy to get blinded by your feelings, and your hormones. I'm not denying they're good-looking boys, but mark my words. They'll lead you down a path you may not want to go on, and once you're down there, there may be no coming back from it. And if there isn't, I might not be able to save you."

I straightened up and looked her right in the eyes. "Maybe I don't want saving."

She looked at me sadly. "Then it might be too late already."

CHAPTER FIFTEEN

KENNEDY

"Ice said you had an idea of how we might be able to deal with Samuel Bell." Mannix wore a pair of shorts and nothing else. His chiselled chest and stomach were slick with sweat. His hair was damp, stuck to his forehead. His face was slightly red, suggesting he'd come from the gym in the back of the house. The one in town was weeks away yet. Maybe longer.

Before I could answer, he grinned and walked over to the side of the pool. He jumped, his knees tucked up to his body, arms around his legs. He landed with a splash so big it threatened to flood over me, even though I was leaning against the far end of the pool.

He surged up to the surface, exploding out of the water like he was the son of Neptune. He shook his hair and face, sending droplets flying. Water cascaded down his chest like a stone waterfall, or something from a movie. If I had a phone in my hand, he'd be my next lockscreen.

He gave me a knowing look and slowly swam over to me, chin bobbing just above the water.

The expression on his face was going to make me flood in a whole different way. He looked like he wanted to bend me over, slam his cock into me and fuck me silly.

My tongue slid over my lips.

"Not so much him as his computer systems." I forced myself to focus in spite of the blood thundering through my brain. Not to mention the rest of my body. Meeting these guys awakened something in me I had no idea existed. I didn't care what Mum said, I couldn't stay away from them if I wanted to.

"I was thinking, I could create a virus that would corrupt all his files. Or better yet, erase them." The headache that would cause him would almost make up for wanting me dead.

Almost.

Mannix smiled and cupped my cheeks in his hands. He wore a massive watch which must have been waterproof, because water dripped off it and he didn't look concerned. If I had to guess, I'd think it was worth a shit ton of money. Probably a drop in the ocean for him, like so many other things around here.

"How long would that take?"

"That depends if you want to scramble everything or delete it altogether. A nasty virus might take me a week or two. Anything more than that will take a lot longer. And it would need a delivery system."

"What sort of delivery system?" He seemed to like the idea.

"Anything from a USB drive, to something that would connect to his systems by Bluetooth. A USB would be faster, but more dangerous because it would have to be done in person. So would Bluetooth, but you wouldn't have to touch anything. Whoever would deliver it would still have to go there in person."

I felt like a spy planning to gain information from some foreign government, not a mobster trying to bring down the enemy. I remembered what Mum said about being morally grey, but as far as I was concerned, this was justice. If we messed with his systems, no one had to die. It seemed like the perfect compromise to me.

Unless he figured out who did it. In which case, we might be slightly fucked. I trusted the guys could do this in a way that wouldn't come back on us.

There was probably a long list of assholes they could blame it on.

Mannix nodded slowly. "How good are you at disabling security systems?" The question was accompanied with another knowing look.

"I wasn't going to sit back and let you lock me in here against my will." I raised my chin. I wasn't going to apologise, but I wondered how he knew I'd fiddled with the code on the gate.

"Lucky guess," he said as though he read my mind. "It's exactly the thing I'd expect my girl to do. Exactly what I would do if I was you." He brushed his lips over mine.

"For what it's worth, it wasn't easy. It took me days just to get into the gate's system, much less mess around with it. If I can get around that, I can get around whatever security Bell has on his house. It would also take time and I'd have to know what he has in place first."

"If I can get you that information, can you get us in?"

"In theory," I said slowly. "It would be a lot riskier than infecting his systems with a virus. I could make it so it plays an obnoxious song whenever anyone tries to boot up a computer." That wouldn't do much damage to anything but his sanity. Unless he liked the song, in which case it would backfire.

Mannix chuckled. "As tempting as that is, that's going to do a short-term amount of damage. Someone like him will have all his shit backed up in seventeen different places. If we're really going to hit him, we need to take out as much as we can. Even if doing it is as risky as hell. What's life without a little risk?"

"Boring." I hadn't seen Ice arrive, but now he was crouched down beside us. Like Mannix, he only wore shorts and a sheen of sweat.

Ares stood right behind him, looking like a blond god.

"Who's boring?" Ares curled his lip in my direction, like they must be talking about me. His attitude towards me had thawed somewhat in the last week or so, but he was still an abrasive asshole.

Still, I couldn't stop thinking about his hands all over my breasts.

I knew he wanted more, but I wouldn't push him.

"Life without risk," Ice said without looking over his shoulder. "What are we risking and when do we leave?" He didn't even know what it was and he was all in.

I admired that about him. That and the way his damp hair coiled around his ears.

"We're risking dying, and not for a few weeks." Mannix raised his face and looked up at both guys. In a handful of words, he explained what we'd talked about.

"I'm in." Ice stood and did a perfect swan dive into the water.

"Sounds like fun." Ares followed him a moment later, so close he almost hit Ice as he resurfaced.

Rather than being mad, Ice laughed. "You're going to have to try harder than that if you're going to sink the Iceman."

"More like Ice*berg*," Ares said. "Always in the way when you're trying to steer your ship around."

Ice frowned at him for a moment. "Is that a euphemism for jerking yourself off? Because it sounds like one."

One of Ares's eyebrows jerked upward. "That sounds accurate, because my cock is the size of the Titanic."

I waited for a beat or two, but none of the guys took the bait so I decided to.

"You realise the Titanic is really small in comparison to modern cruise ships, right?"

He flipped me off. "I meant the Titanic compared to her contemporaries."

"Sure you did." Ice drew out the first word in teasing disbelief. "Also the Titanic is a wreck at the bottom of the ocean, in case you've forgotten."

Ares rolled his eyes and shook his head. "Bro, you're missing the point. The point is—"

"I know what the point is," Ice said. "Your dick is big and fancy. And likes being wet."

"And should probably stay away from Ice," Ares added with a grunt. He started to paddle across to the other side of the pool.

Ice frowned at his back. "Ouch. Lucky I'm the hot kind of ice, not the cold kind."

"Yes, you are," I said to him.

"Definitely," Mannix agreed.

They both locked eyes on each other.

My stomach did a couple of cartwheels and a backsault. Were they about to kiss? My heart raced like crazy at the thought of it.

"Tell us what you want," Mannix whispered, without taking his eyes off Ice.

Was it just that easy?

My tongue darted over my lips.

I started to say, 'Only if you want to,' but stopped

myself. They wanted me to be honest about what I wanted, so that's what I'd give them.

"I want you to kiss each other." Blood pumped so loud in my ears I hardly heard myself speak, but I knew the words came out and were audible, because Mannix put his hands on Ice's shoulders and drew him closer until their chests met.

The first kiss was just a brushing of lips, but soon became deeper, more passionate.

The wet smacking of their mouths was almost enough to make me come on the spot.

And then they were drawing apart, their eyes still on each other.

"I've been wanting to do that for a long time," Ice said softly.

"Me too." Mannix looked at Ice like he hadn't seen him before. Not in this light anyway.

"Did you like that, Princess?" Mannix turned his head slightly to look at me.

I swallowed hard. "I liked that a lot. It was hot, and you two together is... It looks so right."

"It's as right as you with either of us, or both of us." Ice slipped an arm around me and pulled me closer to both of them. "Now if we can just convince Ares."

"Ares will come around in his own time," Mannix said.

We all turned to look over to where Ares swam laps of the pool.

As far as I could tell, they'd all done at least an hour or two of exercise in the gym, and now they were out here doing more. They were nothing if not dedicated to keeping their bodies looking fucking amazing.

I was one hundred percent here for it. That was the reason I was in the pool myself. To exercise and keep fit.

If Ares noticed us watching, he gave no sign. He powered on through the water, arm over arm, over arm. He could have contended with any Olympic swimmer, if he wanted to. I didn't blame him if he didn't. I understood the level of dedication it took to get to a high level of an athlete's chosen sport. I'd opted to focus on my studies and keep gymnastics as a hobby, and I didn't regret that. Even if I was good enough, I wasn't dedicated enough to make it to the top. I preferred to be the top in cybersecurity, and stick to climbing, swinging and tumbling for what spare time I had.

I grabbed Mannix's wrist and looked at his watch.

"I should hop out. I have to interview coaches in an hour." I wished Charlie hadn't turned out to be such a dickhead, because this process was a pain in my ass. What did I know about hiring staff? All I knew was that I wanted someone who wasn't going to try to kill me, or handcuff me to a chair, or hand me over to someone who would kill me, or...

Yeah, it was a long list.

"We're coming with you," Mannix said.

Ice nodded his agreement.

"Maybe I should hire Nicola to run the place while I coach," I said with a sigh. I headed for the ladder to haul myself up out of the water. "How did you get her to sell the place anyway?"

Mannix grinned. "We knew a few things about her she didn't want other people to know about." He was smug as hell.

Whatever it was, it must have been big. She was attached to the place. Did I want to know what she did? As long as it had nothing to do with the children, then probably not. Honestly, if it had anything to do with the children, she'd be dead right now.

I grabbed up my towel. It dangled from my fingers. "You bribed her?"

"I prefer to think of it as gentle persuasion," he said. "Bribery is such an ugly word."

"Since when did you care about words being ugly?" Ice asked him.

"Never," Mannix admitted. "But there's a first time for everything." He gave Ice a glance and I knew he was thinking about their kiss.

"As long as the first isn't the only time," I said.

Ice grinned. "Not a chance. That was the first time of many."

CHAPTER SIXTEEN

ICE

"That's the last of them." Mannix nodded as the fifth potential gymnastics coach headed towards Kennedy's office. Most of them were older students of the gym, or those like Kennedy who used it recreationally. One or two of them were from other places, recently moved to Dusk Bay.

Very recently, judging by the look the fourth one gave us as she stepped towards the door. For some reason, her eyes were wide, nervous.

I couldn't resist sticking my face out towards her and saying, "Boo."

She let out a squeak and scurried out the door.

I chuckled. "I've still got it." I might have flexed.

"Yes, you do." Mannix watched the door until it closed. He had his best, 'don't fuck with me,' expression on his face. He'd walked in the door with it and it hadn't left since.

Personally, I liked it, but for some reason it seemed to intimidate everyone who walked through the door. If they couldn't deal with it now, then they wouldn't stay working here for long.

I leaned back against the wall and crossed my legs at my ankles. "You already know who she should hire, don't you?"

The big question here was, would he give Kennedy a choice? She wanted to run this place her way, and I respected that, but we needed to trust whoever she had working for her. She didn't need another Charlie.

I was still sulking because Mannix wouldn't let me take him down to my workroom. Kennedy didn't need him anymore and he *had* touched her. In my book, that made him a prime candidate for a bit of fun and maybe some experimentation. There was always something to learn when it came to inflicting pain.

"We can still use him," Mannix had said in his stubborn-as-fuck tone. There was no moving him when he was in that frame of mind.

"Use him for what?" Ares asked.

The only reply Mannix would give was to say, "I

have a few things in mind. Ice can have him when I'm finished."

I held out my pinky finger. "Promise?"

Mannix gave me a funny look but hooked my pinky finger with his. "If there's anything left of him, I promise you can have it."

I pumped the air with my fist. "Yes."

In retrospect I shouldn't have gotten so excited, because that was days ago and Charlie was still running around in one piece. And so, the sulking continued.

"Two of them have parents who work for Ric DiMarco," Mannix said. "Of those two, one also drives a delivery van. The other works in a restaurant making pizza. It's a no-brainer."

"Absolutely." I nodded so vigorously I had to check my hair to make sure the bun hadn't come loose. "Pizza maker for the win."

Mannix snorted. "I can see where that would be useful, but a delivery van can go places others can't."

He had a point, but I still liked the idea of having a skilled pizza maker around.

Priorities.

"You know, I don't think Kennedy is taking into consideration her employee's future contribution to the family business," I said. "She might disagree with your assessment."

The idea was to pick a gymnastics coach, not a lackey for Mannix, Leo or Ric. Wasn't it?

"Then we'll have to persuade her," Mannix said reasonably.

"Why do I have the feeling my workroom is going to get really busy, very soon?" I would absolutely not put it past Mannix to dispose of the other candidates just to get his way.

"Because Kennedy's safety is important. Nothing and no one is going to get in the way of that."

"Including Kennedy?" I asked. "Our girl might disagree with that." I knew she knew how important her safety was. I saw that in the way she quickly and easily slipped into the role when Nixon was chained to the ceiling. The way she embraced her darkness was one of the hottest things I've ever seen. Followed closely by watching her fuck Mannix and Ares while I tortured the man.

I saw the darkness in her the first time we met, but now she was coming to see it. I loved every minute of it.

"Let me worry about that." Mannix was silent for a minute or two before he broke it by saying, "About that kiss."

I hadn't expected him to bring it up, but now he did, I was slightly worried.

"You don't regret it, do you?" I hadn't had to deal with rejection very often. I wasn't good at it. People tended to get hurt while I worked through my frustration. I was okay with that, but they weren't.

"No." His reply wasn't quick, but it was firm. "Just making sure you don't."

I'd never seen uncertainty on his face, and it was only a flash, but it was there.

Exploiting vulnerabilities was one of my superpowers, but I wouldn't do it with Mannix. Or anyone I cared about. The feeling it gave me was conflicting. I wasn't used to it from him and it threw me off a little bit. If anything, it made me like him even more.

Who knew there was an actual person with feelings under his rock hard façade?

"I have absolutely no regrets." I pushed myself up off the wall and stepped over to give him an awkward bro hug. I'd kissed him and I'd had his cock down my throat, but I wasn't used to actual affection with another guy. Hugging, snuggling, that was out of my wheelhouse, but I was willing to learn.

"Actually, I have one," I said. I looked for the flicker of uncertainty again, but it wasn't there. His stoic-as-fuck mask was back in place. In case there was some misery, I decided to put him out of it.

"I wish we did it sooner, and I hope we can do more of it."

His brief nod was the only sign of his relief. He put a hand on the back of my head and spoke in a whisper.

"You should know that, as far as I'm concerned, you're mine, as much as Kennedy is. If anyone touches either of you, unless it's Ares, I'll rip off their faces and make them eat it."

I whispered back. "That is so fucking hot. Also, I'd like to see that. How would you keep them alive long enough for them to eat their own face?"

He sounded like he almost choked on a laugh. "That's your department, I just make the threats."

I smiled. "Got it." Of course now my mind was in a whirl, thinking how to do just that for him. With any luck, I could try it on Charlie soon.

"If anyone touches you or Kennedy, unless it's Ares, I get to use my chair." I kept my chair for extra special occasions. As fun as it was to chain people to the ceiling, the chair was more personal. It let me get down to their level. Also, with their feet restrained, I got to do all sorts of interesting things to their toes.

They were fascinating thing, toes. Sensitive,

often ticklish, and beautifully protected by nails. Until they weren't.

I could spend days playing with people's feet and never get tired of it.

"What happens if anyone touches Ares?" I jerked my head towards the new gym, where he was currently overlooking the renovation. He seemed to have taken it on as his own personal project. No one seemed to mind, so we left him to it.

"He punches them out," Mannix said. "Failing that, I'm sure we can think of some suitable punishment for them."

"Maybe we could set up that workroom out in the Simpson desert like we talked about," I said. I was curious to see how people would cope when being restrained and tortured out in the desert, under the relentless Australian sun. I suspected it would suck really hard. For them. And for me, because I hated extreme heat like that. Still, it would be worth it.

"We could buy an island and you could use the beach for that," Mannix said distractedly.

I followed his gaze and watched the fifth interviewee leave Kennedy's office and head for the door.

He gave us an uneasy look before he hurried out.

"I don't like the idea of any men working here," I remarked.

"There's going to be men working next door during and after the renovation," Mannix pointed out. "Although there are several women tradies in there now."

"We could make it a women-only gym." That would circumvent any drama with other men being near Kennedy.

"Then we couldn't use it." Still, Mannix looked like he was considering the idea.

"Then we make it women and us only." That was a simple enough solution as far as I was concerned.

"Let's see how we go when it's finished."

"Is it too late to change and make it a ballet studio instead? There would be fewer men there then." I'd still use it, because I quite enjoyed ballet when I was a kid. I never cared that some people thought it was a girly thing to do. It was hard work and it was fun, and I enjoyed being one of only two boys amongst all those girls.

"Or a beauty salon." I frowned. "Never mind. Guys would go there for their back, crack and sack wax. That would be much worse."

"Yeah, much," Mannix agreed. "That's something Kennedy doesn't need to see or think about."

"What do I not need to see or think about?" Kennedy stepped out of her office in time to hear his last comment.

"Other men's balls," I said lightly. "We were talking about what would happen if other guys were around here."

She gave me a funny look, like she couldn't quite put the presence of other guys, and her seeing their balls, together.

Fair enough, out of context it probably seemed like a strange thing to be talking about. On the other hand, we were us and strange was what we did. Okay, it was what *I* did, but the other guys went along with it most of the time.

Before she could figure it out, Mannix spoke.

"You're hiring the second one." He didn't even try to phrase it as a question. It was a statement he expected to be a fact. There wasn't even a millimetre of leeway or indecision. His face was somehow even more stony than usual.

Predictably, Kennedy looked annoyed.

"Am I?" She managed to keep her tone light, but it came with an audible bristle. "I didn't realise you interviewed them all before they got here."

Mannix gave her a look past his eyebrows. One slightly tinged with disbelief.

"We thoroughly vetted them long before they walked through the door. If they hadn't passed that, none of them would be here. The second one is the most suitable." He wasn't budging.

Neither was she. "I haven't made my mind up yet. When I do I'll—"

He caught her wrist and pulled her until they were chest to chest. "You'll hire the second one," he said again. "Otherwise the other four won't be around to be options."

"Are you threatening me?" She looked up at him, her gaze unwavering.

His eyebrows dropped. "No. I'm threatening *them*. The second one, Greta Ferguson, is qualified, experienced and has a job which brings references. All of those references back up the choice. The only reason she wasn't working here already, was because her parents' interests clashed with Nicola's."

"She was nice," Kennedy conceded. "I was leaning towards her anyway."

Mannix smiled. "Good." He loosened his grip on her wrist and tugged her in for a long, slow kiss. "You can tell her this afternoon."

No one was as smug as Mannix when he got his way, not even Ares.

Kennedy, on the other hand, looked slightly less

impressed. I had no doubt she would hire Greta, but only because she wanted to. Pleasing Mannix was an added bonus.

I think the only one who didn't realise that was him.

CHAPTER SEVENTEEN

"How's the virus going?"

Of all the people to take an interest, I was surprised it was Ares.

All the guys had a vested interest, but he was the one to ask.

Specifically, I was surprised he chose to talk to me. He barely said two words to me since that day down in the workroom. If I thought he was distant before, then he was even more so now. He didn't even bother to smirk or curl his lip at me. In fact, he seemed to be trying hard to avoid me. That was difficult when we were all living under the same roof, but he managed it most of the time.

When he actually asked me a question, it took a couple of moments before I could answer.

"It's almost ready," I replied. "With everything that's going on, and trying to keep up with my studies, I haven't had as much time as I'd hoped, but it's nearly there."

Now that Greta had settled into her new second job—she was going to keep driving her courier van as well—things started to calm down somewhat.

He stepped further into the study and looked over my shoulder, at the screen.

"Looks like a cat walked on a keyboard."

I think he meant it as an insult, but I laughed. "It does, doesn't it? If I asked my computer to read it out loud, it wouldn't know what to make of it. But if I fed it into another computer, it would screw it up."

"That's the idea, isn't it?" He pulled over another chair and straddled it backwards, his arms resting on the back of the chair.

"Basically, but at this point they could clean it up. If it could get past their security systems. There's a way to go before it'll do what we want it to do."

"Sounds like fucking with people's heads is easier than fucking with their computers." His eyes went from the screen to me.

"Probably. Modern computer systems are designed so people can't get past them with things like this. Human brains are both more complex and more simple."

"That's true," he agreed. "It's easy to mess with people and scare them, but wiping all the information that's in there..." He tapped the side of his head with the tip of his finger.

"That's a virtual impossibility. Especially when it comes to forgetting things we want to forget. That stuff is harder to dislodge than most things."

"Are you speaking from experience?" I asked gently. If he wanted to open up to me, I'd give him the chance to do that.

For a moment, I thought he might actually tell me, but then his expression shut right down, tighter than ever.

"We all have baggage. I bet you still remember that night in the forest after the masked ball. The way you felt when we appeared. Or did you stumble on us when we were already there?" He didn't give me a chance to answer.

"Do you think about the way Mannix sliced open Eric's throat? The way Ice stabbed him in the eye while I held him down so he couldn't run? Do Ice's words haunt your dreams, little mouse?"

In spite of myself, I shivered.

"I think about all of those things. Even knowing

what I know now, it still gives me the creeps." It most likely always would.

I found my arms wrapped around myself. "Why are you asking about it?"

He smiled, clearly pleased he got to me the way he had.

"Just making sure you haven't forgotten what we're all capable of." He sat up and stared me down.

"I was there in the warehouse, remember?" I managed to keep my voice even. "I think you're saying that because you're scared."

He scoffed. "What do I have to be scared about, little mouse?"

I leaned towards him. "I think you want to fuck with my head because you're scared to fuck with my body. I think you're pissed off at yourself for touching me the other day. I think you're even more pissed off because you want to do it again. And again."

I moved closer. "And again."

His hand shot out and wrapped around my throat. His eyes were like chips of blue ice.

"Grinding against you one time doesn't mean I want to do it again. I got caught in the moment. All that blood, all that *pain*. It made my balls so heavy, my cock so hard. I needed release and you were there. That was it. Don't read more into it than there is."

I met his gaze. "Did you know choking is the new dozen roses?" His hand around my throat made me wet as hell. "Doing it just means you care."

His fingers tightened.

I had to suppress a moan. If he pulled me onto the top of the desk and fucked me, I'd be one hundred percent into it.

We both knew it.

He dropped his hand. "I wouldn't want you to think I care, when I don't." His tone was harsh, but rough with need.

I couldn't see past the back of the chair. I didn't need to. I knew his cock would be rock hard. I tried not to picture it, or imagine how it would feel if he slid it inside my body.

"Did you study delusion at uni? Because I know you don't hate me as much as you pretend to."

"Maybe I hate you more." He shifted uncomfortably in his seat. "I might be pretending to be nice once in a while to keep the peace."

If that was the case, he wasn't good at it. Or maybe he had different ideas of being nice than I did. Mine usually didn't involve sneering, smirking and generally being an asshole.

I cocked my head. "I don't think you hate me at all. I think maybe for some reason, you hate yourself, but I don't think you hate me. No more than you hate Mannix or Ice."

"Why would I hate myself? I'm hot, smart and awesome." He smirked.

I wasn't going to feed his already inflated ego by agreeing with him.

"I don't know," I admitted. "Maybe because you don't have the same power Mannix does, or his father does. Maybe because you don't get to slice people up the way Ice does. Maybe for some other reason. Were you not cuddled enough as a kid?"

His eyes flicked to the side and I knew I hit a nerve.

"You know, whatever you need, we're here for you," I said gently. "You don't always have to put up the tough guy act."

That brought his chin up. "Who says it's an act?"

"I haven't studied as much psychology as you have, but it's always an act," I said. "Underneath every exterior is a vulnerable person. Even yours. Even Mannix and Ice. Even me."

"It's not an act." His chin dipped slightly.

There was definitely a scared little boy under there somewhere. He'd lived so long in an environment where you don't show fear, in case someone used it against you. He'd suppressed it like the others had, but it was there.

What would it take to bring it out the rest of the way? And would he hate me if I saw it? Legitimately hate me, I mean.

I shrugged. "If you say so."

"I do say so. I'm starting to think I was right about you. You're a pain in the ass."

"Funny, I was thinking the same about you." He liked to think he was a big, bad, tough dude, and he was, but deep down there was a lot more to Ares Turner than he showed people.

He grunted. "I didn't hear you complaining about what I was doing to your ass the other day. In fact, you seemed to be enjoying yourself. Did you like the way I touched your tits? I know I left bruises on them."

I quickly glanced down and then back up again.

"I did like it," I said. "But the bruises have almost gone."

He glanced down too. "Shame. I must not have applied enough pressure. They should have lasted much longer than that."

I waited until he looked back up to speak again. "You'd like to leave more on them, wouldn't you? You get pleasure out of giving other people pain. Do you like getting it in return? Do you like being spanked, or do you want to be the one doing the spanking?"

The way his pupils contracted was all the answer I needed.

He leaned forward again. "If I spanked you, the bruises would last a lot longer. You'd be lucky if you could sit down for a month."

I leaned forward too, until our noses were almost close enough to brush against each other.

When I spoke, my voice was as rough as his was a couple of minutes earlier.

"Don't threaten me with a good time."

He looked straight into my eyes. His breath was on my lips.

I breathed it in. The taste it left on my tongue was warm, like cum, honey and coffee all mixed together.

"How wet are you?" he whispered.

"Drenched," I whispered back. "Dripping." If I wasn't careful, I was going to have a trickle of slick down the inside of my thighs. "How hard are you?"

"Like a fucking rock," he admitted. "You're going to be the death of me. You piss me off more than anyone I've ever met, but I also want to fuck you more than anyone else. But I'm not going to."

"You're not?" There wasn't more than a hair or two between our lips. One movement, one bump and we'd kiss.

"No. When I fuck you, it's going to be something you'll never forget. I'll paddle your ass until you scream and beg me to slam my cock into you. I'm going to give you more pleasure and pain than you ever imagined. When I'm done with you, you'll be nothing more than a puddle. You won't be able to walk for days. You're going to feel me for weeks."

I was already almost a puddle just from his words. These guys were going to be the absolute end of me. And I couldn't wait.

We sat like that for at least a few minutes more, inhaling and swallowing each other's breaths. When I thought he might give in and kiss me anyway, he sat up, away from me.

He gave me a look like he couldn't believe he'd said any of that, and he was angry with me for—I don't know what. Hearing it? Making him say it, although I didn't?

Whatever it was, I felt like we were right back at the start again. Or close enough to it anyway. Whatever walls he'd lowered slightly, he shoved back up into place. I could almost see him locking them and throwing away the key.

"You should hurry up with that virus." He was all businesslike now. It was almost as though the time between his first question and now didn't exist. Didn't happen at all. Like the only conversation we had was about the virus and the plan to go after Samuel Bell.

"I could if I wasn't being distracted," I retorted. If he was going to behave like nothing passed between us, then so would I.

"I'll get out of here then, little mouse," he said mockingly. He got up off the chair and started towards the door.

I turned back to my computer, but before he could leave I said, "You said *when* you fuck me, not *if.*"

He stopped in the doorway for a few beats, then stalked away.

CHAPTER EIGHTEEN

"You're going to need this." Mannix held a dress bag over his arm as he stepped into the room and closed the door behind him.

We'd arrived in Sydney that morning, on the first flight out of Dusk Bay. Mannix only told us last night that we were coming at all. He'd hustled us on and off the plane and into a small hotel. It was the kind of place where none of the staff asked any questions, or paid much attention to people's comings and goings.

It was also the kind of place visitors shouldn't ask too many questions, because the carpet was stained, and so were the quilts covering both beds. I decided against peeling back the sheets to see what state they were in.

"When did you have time to organise this?" I slid

the zipper aside far enough to reveal black silk. He'd only popped out of the room for about five minutes.

He shrugged one shoulder. "I organised it after I booked our flights. It should fit you." He nodded to the other guys and started to pull his own suit out of his suitcase.

Ice and Ares would wear the same suits they wore to Mum and Leo's wedding. Mannix wore a similar one, but in dark grey. Each of the guys wore a tie that matched their personalities. Mannix's was a couple of shades darker than his suit. Ares' was black. Ice's tie was brightly coloured, but mostly red.

"Try it on," Ice said.

I drew the zipper down all the way and pulled out the dress to slip it on. It fell to just above my knees. Spaghetti straps held the fitted bodice in place. The rest of the dress clung to my curves like a second skin.

"You look hot." Ice pulled up the zipper and nuzzled his face into my hair. "I'm starting to think you shouldn't go."

"She definitely shouldn't," Ares said with a grunt. "It's too big a risk to take someone who doesn't know what they're doing."

"Then you better not go, because I'm the one who knows how to activate the virus," I retorted.

"You could tell one of us." He matched my tone. "You're not the only one who can—"

"Enough," Mannix snapped. "We're all going. We only need to blend in long enough to do what needs to be done and then we get the fuck out of there. Samuel Bell should be busy playing the dutiful host, and most of the people won't know what we look like."

"It's the people who do know what we look like that I'm worried about," Ares said. "If anyone from Brutham is there—"

"We do the best we fucking can to avoid them." Mannix fixed him with a firm look. "This isn't our first rodeo. We all know what we need to do. We go in, do it and get out."

"Can we have a drink before we leave?" Ice asked.

Mannix's response was to shake his head. "We can get shitfaced afterwards."

Ice pumped the air with his fist. "Hell yeah."

"Wait until we have something to celebrate," Ares told him.

"I always have something to celebrate, I'm me." Ice grinned.

Ares gave him the side eye and a snort. "Whatever you say, bro."

Ice clapped him on the shoulder, hard enough to hurt judging by the expression on Ares' face.

"I do say," Ice said.

I tuned out their banter as I slipped my feet into a pair of heels. I twisted my hair into a neat bun and pinned it into place.

I felt sexy. Mannix couldn't have made a better choice. It seemed as though he knew me better than my mother did, or at least he had better taste.

I couldn't dismiss the possibility he saw the darkness in me and matched the dress to it. I hadn't exactly tried to hide it from him or the other guys. They got me like no one else ever had. For the first time in my life, I felt like I didn't have to hide.

"We could do rock, paper, scissors," Ice was saying when I tuned back in.

"What are you competing over?" I asked.

"Who's going to take that dress off you when this is finished," Ice said with a shit-eating grin.

Yeah, I should have guessed.

"Shouldn't we be going?" I picked up my phone and the USB, and raised my perfectly plucked eyebrows at the guys.

"I'd rather be coming, but let's get this done." Ice offered me his arm.

Mannix narrowed his eyes at him, but stepped out the door in front of us. Ares walked behind.

"That's not a limo," Ice remarked as we stepped out the front of the hotel toward a dark grey sedan.

"The idea is to blend in at old man Bell's party," Mannix said. "A limo would stand out like dogs' balls."

"Or mine." Ice grabbed his groin. "Mine stand out more than any dog I've ever seen."

"That's only because your cock is so small it makes your balls look big," Ares remarked.

"That sounds like jealousy talking to me," Ice told him.

Ares barked a laugh and slipped into the passenger seat beside the driver. He muttered something about Ice being delusional and pulled the door closed behind him.

Ice chuckled and gestured for me to sit in the middle between him and Mannix.

Mannix leaned forward and spoke to the driver, his voice too soft for me to hear. The driver nodded a couple of times and pulled the car away from the curb.

"It should only take us about ten minutes to get there, depending on traffic." Mannix sat back like a prince in his royal carriage. "Are you ready?"

I toyed with the USB stick, but nodded. "I think so. I mean, we've gone over this a hundred times, but there's still a lot that could go wrong. This—" I held up the stick, "should work perfectly."

I hoped.

It was everything else we could fuck up. So many variables we couldn't possibly account for.

"It'll be fine," Ice said. "Better than fine. It'll be *fun*. What could be better than inviting ourselves to a fancy party held by our enemy?" He sounded like he was ready to have the time of his life. Knowing Ice, that was exactly what he planned to do.

"Just about anything," I said. "If they catch us—"

"They won't catch us," Mannix said firmly. "We planned out every detail. Everything should go smoothly. And if it doesn't, we'll deal with it. Don't worry, we've got you. Your job is to get in, do what you need to do and get out. And look hot doing it."

He made it sound so easy I almost relaxed, but I kept turning the USB around and around in my hand.

Mannix caught my chin between his thumb and forefinger and turned my face towards him.

"Do you trust us?" He looked at me intently, searching for an honest response in my eyes.

"I trust you," I said softly. I did, but I was scared.

It all seemed so easy when we were planning everything, but now, it was getting more and more real by the moment. Was it too late to turn back and go home? No one had to know we were ever there.

"Then trust that we know what we're doing. We'll be in and out in less than ten minutes, and no one will know we were there. When we're done, it'll take Samuel Bell a decade to fix what we've done. Reuben Brantley might even give us a medal." He grinned.

As far as I could tell, Reuben Brantley didn't give medals, but his opinion was clearly important to the guys. In their world—*our* world—the kind of power that might be bestowed on them by Brantley was everything. If we succeeded tonight, the impact would last for years.

If we failed, the four of us would end up dead, or worse. I didn't let myself think about what might happen. Whatever it was, it wouldn't be pretty for anyone.

"What does Leo think about this?" I hadn't seen him or Mum before we left.

Mannix's eyes flicked away from me, evasively. "He doesn't know. I spoke to Ric DiMarco about it. He supplied the car and the money for your dress. He has faith that we'll succeed."

I blinked at him a couple of times. "You went over your father's head?"

He placed a hand on my thigh, and slid it up under the hem of my dress.

"If we don't succeed, no one can blame my father. And if we do succeed, then he can't take the credit."

I suspected the latter was the point. Mannix wanted to own this operation. To use it to make a name for himself. I wasn't going to judge him for that. We all wanted to stand on our own two feet, independent of our parents.

This was exactly the kind of thing my mother warned me about when she suggested the guys were trouble. If she knew about this, she'd be worried at best and furious at worst.

Especially if she knew it was my idea.

Not the party, as such, but the virus. Given a chance, I might have thought of coming here tonight, while Bell was distracted with the festivities, instead of Mannix.

Maybe the guys' mothers should be warning them about me.

"Is Leo going to be pissed off at us?" I asked.

Regardless of Mannix's reasons for doing things the way he did, I didn't want my stepfather angry with me. That may lead to friction between him and Mum. I didn't want to be the cause of any problems between them. Although, at this point, my mother would take Leo's side over mine. While that thought should sting, I'd take the guy's side over hers in a bunch of things, including me staying in Dusk Bay and not fleeing somewhere that may or may not be safer.

"Only if we fail," Mannix said. "Then he'll distance himself from us and all of this as quickly as he can."

I could totally see that. Leo would do whatever he had to do to cover his own ass.

I glanced out the window to see the lights of the city flash past. I hadn't realised how much I missed Sydney until now. Dusk Bay was a smaller city, without the huge glass-sided skyscrapers and historic buildings. Both were just as gritty and busy, but Dusk Bay didn't have the harbour. The bay wasn't anywhere near as magnificent or as big. The water-front houses were similar in both places though. Large, opulent and expensive.

We pulled up under a tree, a dark car amidst the shadows. There wasn't even a streetlight to illuminate us here. Once the driver turned off the headlights, we blended into the night.

A shiver of apprehension trickled down my spine. It ratcheted up to anxiety as I followed Mannix out of the car. The full smells and sounds of the city hit me the moment my heels touch the ground. Salt air, exhaust fumes, traffic, music from the nearby party. It was an assault on my senses, spiking my nerves.

"Are you sure this is a good idea?" I said as Mannix closed the car door behind us. "A cyber attack from a distance would be—"

"Not as much fun." Ice slipped his hand into mine. "You said this should be more effective, and what could be better than a direct attack on Samuel Bell? Knowing someone was inside his house will freak him the fuck out." He grinned.

"Don't forget he wants you dead," Mannix said. "He's getting what he deserves."

Before I could think of another argument or say another word, Mannix led the way up the leafy street.

After another moment of hesitation, we followed behind him.

CHAPTER NINETEEN

KENNEDY

As planned, the party was in full swing when we stepped up to the house. Mannix flashed a fake invitation and a smile at the security guard on the gate. She didn't seem impressed by his smile, but she nodded at the invitation and waved us through.

"You can't please everyone," he muttered as we stepped away towards the house.

"You better not try, or Kennedy and I will remove your toenails, one by one," Ice told him.

"Or his fingernails," I agreed jokingly. Or maybe I wasn't joking.

The thought of Mannix with anyone else ignited a bonfire of jealousy inside me. If any of the guys touched another woman, I might scratch her eyes out. These guys were mine.

"As if I'd go there with anyone else," Mannix said. "I have everything I need already."

He nodded for us to be quiet, while we stepped around the curved driveway and through the wide open front doors.

The sound of music and voices came from somewhere at the back of the house.

"Pool area." Ares nodded in that direction. "It also has a harbour view. This place is worth a shit ton of money. It used to be worth more, but a house down the street disappeared into a sinkhole a couple of years ago. Fucked with property value for a while there." His tone didn't even hold a slight hint of sympathy. If anything, he sounded pleased.

"I remember that," I said. "They never could figure out why a sinkhole opened right there."

Ares shrugged. "Yeah, whatever. That's another thing on a long list of things I don't give a shit about. Although, the owner of that house was smokin' hot."

I gave him a look which he returned with an even gaze. We'd barely spoken since the conversation we shared. Sometimes he looked like he was ready to say something civil. Most of the time he seemed more pissed off than usual, on the verge of telling me to fuck off.

I shrugged it off each time. When he was ready

to talk, we could talk. Until then, he could keep on acting like he didn't give a shit. We both knew he did.

"The office should be over here." Mannix nodded toward the east and skirted around a handful of partygoers. No one gave him, or any of us, a second glance.

"I'd kill for a drink," Ice said loudly. "Do you think they have decent beer here?"

"Haven't you had enough?" Ares asked. Our cover story was that we came from another party, which was why we arrived late. People were more likely to avoid us if they thought we were already drunk.

In theory anyway.

"No way." Ice exaggeratedly waved his arm in the air. "I'm just getting started."

Mannix gave them both a look and led us over to a tall, wooden door. A keypad was set into the wall beside it.

He nodded to me and stepped to one side.

I turned on my phone and tapped in the command to disable the lock. It was connected to the house's Wi-Fi system. A few keystrokes later and I'd hacked into that to make it less secure. It was a simple matter to take control of the system after that. I could unlock almost anything in the house, and even send Samuel Bell on a wild goose chase with the GPS in his car. Lucky for him, we weren't here for any of those things.

Not today anyway.

The keypad flashed green and Mannix opened the door. He waved us inside and closed it behind him.

"That was easy." Ice smiled.

"Don't say shit like that." Ares scowled at him. "That's when things start to turn to crap."

We waited, but no one came running.

"Let's get this done." Mannix pointed in the direction of the computer sitting on the wide, timber desk.

The desk alone must have been worth a few thousand dollars. The art on the walls which I looked at with the light on my phone, would have been worth a few million. It was a shame to have them locked away in here where no one but Samuel Bell could enjoy them.

People like him didn't think it was a shame. He probably got a kick out of seeing things no one else could.

I booted up the computer and slid the USB into the slot on the side. Thank fuck Bell still had the kind of computer that took a USB. Otherwise I would have had to deliver the whole virus via Wi-Fi and that would have taken longer.

Who knew when he might get the sudden urge to go into his office to do something? Having to wait for the USB was going to be excruciating enough. Wi-Fi would take at least twice as long, depending on how good the signal was.

This whole operation was nuts as fuck as it was.

I asked myself again why I was here, but the answer was the same every time. Frank Nixon would have strangled me because Samuel Bell wanted him to. That was a good enough reason for this as far as I was concerned.

I tapped the keyboard and got the code rolling into the system, then leaned against the desk to wait, my hip pressed to the expensive wood.

"How long will this take?" Mannix asked. He looked agitated now. Even more than I felt. We'd all breathe easier when we weren't here in this house anymore.

"Approximately five and a half minutes." I glanced at the screen on my phone. I had tried to get it down to closer to three minutes, but it was what it was. If it did what we wanted it to do, it would take the time it took. In the long run, it would be worth it.

I fucking hoped.

"Perfect." He placed his hands around my waist and lifted me onto an empty part of the desk.

"What are you doing?" I said with a nervous laugh.

"I'm going to see which will finish first, your program or you." He grinned and shoved the hem of my skirt up my thighs. In the light from the computer screen, he pushed aside my panties and started to run his fingers over my pussy.

"I don't know if this is the time or place—" My breath gave me away by hitching as the pad of his thumb ghosted over my clit.

Or I could just roll with it, because he had me going like crazy, and the idea of being fucked on Samuel Bell's desk was insanely, intoxicatingly hot. The man tried to kill me, he deserved to have his desk messed up.

"Why didn't I think of that?" Ice grumbled.

"Because I'm the brains of the operation." Mannix grinned at him.

"Sure, let's go with that." Undeterred, Ice peeled down the front of my dress and leaned in to trace his tongue around my nipple.

Heat and fire replaced anxiety, which coursed through my body like a sudden inferno. Figures I'd be turned on here. Anyone could walk in at any moment and find us. We could be dead in the next sixty seconds, but I was as aroused as fuck.

Death, danger and these guys were becoming my aphrodisiac.

I glanced over to see Ares, a dark shape against the door. He seemed to be watching silently. In that case, we'd give him a show.

Mannix pulled me so my ass was on the edge of the desk, then laid me back. Ice moved around to the side of the desk, licking and sucking like I hadn't moved.

Mannix finger fucked me hard, determined, relentless. His fingers sank in and out of my slick heat, the heel of his hand rubbing up and down my clit.

Between them and the excitement of the moment, I felt like I might go absolutely crazy.

Approximately two and a half minutes later, I tipped over the edge to oblivion. I bit my lip hard to keep from screaming out. The last thing we needed was me to give us away by coming too loudly.

Mannix undid his suit trousers and freed his erection before gripping my hips and pulling my legs up around his waist.

"Bro, do we have time—" Ares started.

Mannix interrupted him by slamming his cock

deep into my body, all the way to the hilt. He fucked me the same way he finger fucked me, hard, fast and relentless.

I bit back a cry at the sudden fullness and violence of his body meeting mine.

Ice covered the rest of the cry with his mouth, kissing me deeply while his hands explored my bare breast.

Mannix took about as long as I did before he stilled and came, lips pressed together to keep himself quiet. He grunted, long and low, panted then grunted again.

"Fuck," he whispered. "You're such a fucking good girl." He slid out of me slowly and tugged my panties back into place. He helped me to sit back up and fix my dress. "How long have we got?"

I blinked to clear my head and looked at my phone screen. "About twenty seconds."

He chuckled. "Perfect." He did up his pants and tucked his shirt back into place.

I watched the code roll by and counted the time down in my head. It actually took eighteen and a half seconds, but close enough.

"It's done." I tugged the USB out of the side of the computer and turned the computer off. "The next time someone turns it on, the virus will spread and fry the system. Hopefully, by then, we'll be long gone."

With the party on tonight, it seemed like a reasonable guess that Samuel Bell wouldn't be back in his office until tomorrow, if not Monday morning. By then we'd be comfortably back in Dusk Bay.

Hopefully.

Mannix placed a hand on either side of my face and kissed me hard. "You're incredible."

"Hell yeah I am," I said jokingly. "Let's get out of here." My pussy was throbbing from the way he fucked me, but I could still walk. Or run if I had to.

"Good idea," Ares said. "It might be the first one I've heard come out of your mouth." After a moment he had to concede a little more. "And the virus. But we'll see how well that works." Yeah, he wasn't good at conceding.

"It'll be amazing," I assured him. I stayed back with Mannix and Ice while Ares eased the door open.

We stood in the darkness and watched and listened. After a moment or two, we heard voices approaching.

Two men walked past, talking low to each other. If they noticed the open door, they gave no sign.

They kept walking until they disappeared in the direction of the party.

"Looks clear to me," Ares said.

He led the way out the door and back the way we came, towards the front of the house.

Like on the way in, the front doors to the house were open and no one was around. The closest voices were several metres away at most. Figures moved around the garden, wavy ghosts as the party lights turned them into twisting and turning shapes. The lights strobed in time to the music, corrupting the forms even further.

Reasoning that if we couldn't see them clearly, they couldn't see us either, we hurried across the front lawn and into the darkness of the trees beside the driveway.

We were almost to the gate when a voice said, "What the fuck are you doing here?"

CHAPTER TWENTY

ICE

I managed to keep my cool and contain my surprise. Without even trying to hide it, I put myself between them and Kennedy.

Mannix and Ares both did the same. A wall of awesomeness between her and them.

"The question is, what are you doing here?" I drawled. In the glow of the streetlight, I recognised the Brantley twins. Identical, I could never work out which of the fuckers was which. I knew the woman they were with though.

Interesting.

"I believe we asked first, didn't we Parker?" He must have been Hunter. He looked over at his twin, who had put himself between us and their woman.

Judging by the fact they both wore jeans and t-shirts, they weren't here for the party.

"Yeah, we did," Parker agreed. "Since when did people like you get invited here?"

I didn't know if I should take offence at that or not, but I decided to. Or at least, pretend to.

"People like us? What do you mean by that, exactly?"

"People who aren't on the side of Samuel Bell," Parker said slowly, as though he was talking to a kid.

"Which brings us back to why the fuck are you here?" Mannix asked. He dropped his head to the side and looked around Parker. "Are the evil twins trying to kidnap Chloe Bell?"

"I'm Lila, you idiot." She stepped out from behind Parker. "I look nothing like my sister."

"You're also twins," I pointed out.

She rolled her eyes at him. "No shit, fuckwit, but we're not identical."

I leaned towards her, not bothering to be offended by her calling me names. "You look the same in the dark."

Hunter and Parker did identical twin bristles until Lila snorted.

"As if I'd be in the dark with someone like you."

I smiled. "Right back at you." I wouldn't turn my

back on a woman like her. Especially one who clearly came with a sharpened set of claws.

"You still haven't answered the question," Mannix said. "What are the Brantley twins doing with one of the Bell sisters?"

"Would you believe we're trying to build bridges?" Hunter asked. He glanced at Lila and Parker. "We don't believe the Brantleys and the Bells have to keep being enemies. If we can figure out a way to—"

"So you're fucking?" Ares asked. "Let me guess, if your brother," he gestured at the twins, "and your father," then at Lila, "found out about this, they'd be pissed."

All three of them looked cagey as hell.

"That looks like a yes to me," I remarked.

Hunter leaned to the side to look around me. "Are you going to introduce us to your friend?" His brow creased like he was trying to decide if he knew her or not, but he clearly didn't.

I took Kennedy's hand and tugged her gently so she was beside me, but kept an arm around her.

"This is Kennedy Knight. She's Helen Knight-Cassani's daughter."

"Leo's stepdaughter?" Lila looked Kennedy up and down.

Kennedy looked back at her with open suspicion. "She's a Bell?" she asked me.

I could see the cogs and wheels turning in her brain, thinking about the implication of one of the Bell family seeing us out here.

"Imagine that," Lila sneered. "A Bell outside my own home."

"In the company of two of your father's mortal enemies," Mannix said. "What would he think if he knew?"

"More to the point, what would he *do* if he knew?" I asked.

"The same thing he'd do to you if he knew you were here," Hunter said. "So I propose a deal. You don't say anything about us being here and we won't tell him we saw you."

"If you agree that you don't tell *anyone* you saw us here, we have a deal." Mannix held his hand out to Hunter.

Of course, it would be Mannix who picked up on that little loophole.

Hunter knew it too, I saw it on his face. He hesitated for half a second, then took Mannix's hand and shook it.

"I agree it would be mutually beneficial if no one

knew any of us was here. None of us will say a word to anyone."

I wondered if Lila would agree if she knew what she was agreeing to. Once she realised she couldn't access social media via her family's Wi-Fi, she might regret going along with this. Then again, she was a Bell. She'd probably renege on it the first chance she got. Whatever, as long as we were a long way from here when that happened.

"You really believe there can be peace between the two families?" Kennedy asked, her expression tentative.

I understood her reason for asking. Samuel Bell would be a lot less likely to want her, or any of us, dead if we were one big happy family.

"We know we're not giving Lila up," Parker said. "Whatever it takes to live our lives together, we'll do it. Even if we have to disappear."

Poor bastard, they were more than likely to disappear if Samuel Bell found out they were fucking his daughter. That shit would end up worse than Romeo and Juliet.

I put that into the, 'not my problem,' basket and shoved it out of my mind. No doubt they'd eventually realise they had no chance of making it work and they'd all get on with their lives.

Ares muttered something about guys thinking with their cocks. He shook his head and spoke again, this time loud enough for all of us to hear. "We should get the fuck out of here. We've had enough of this party."

"Yeah, let's go," Mannix said. He jerked his head roughly in the direction of the car.

"You didn't tell us why you were here," Parker said before we could take more than a couple of steps.

"We didn't, did we?" I asked. I looked at him contemplatively for a moment, before I shrugged and followed the others into the darkness. I glanced back over my shoulder, but the twins and Lila didn't follow.

"They're not supposed to be together?" Kennedy asked softly.

"Not even a little bit," I agreed. "They must have snuck over, hoping no one would notice because they're too busy with her old man's party." I had to give them some credit. They had the balls to do something like that.

"Lila and her sister Chloe are in their first year at Brutham," Mannix said. "The twins are in their second year. We helped the twins get through the trials last year. It never hurts to have a Brantley owe you a favour or two."

Kennedy glanced back. "They're Zeke Brantley's brothers?"

I'd forgotten she was a big fan of Wolf Venom. "Yes, they are. There doesn't seem to be much love lost between them though. I wouldn't ask the twins to get you his autograph. They might do it, but they'd want something in return. Trust me, you don't want to owe the evil twins any favours."

"Evil twins?" she echoed. "They don't seem so bad. They seemed interested in making peace between the two groups of mobsters."

"They're interested in taking care of their own hide," Mannix said scathingly. "They work for their brother, Reuben, and as far as I can tell, there's nothing they won't do for him. Including kill you if he decides he wants you dead. They wouldn't even blink."

"Kennedy isn't going to give Reuben a reason to want her dead," I said firmly. "Once word gets out about the virus, he'll be impressed. He might even wish he'd thought of it sooner."

Things like this usually weren't Reuben's method. If he thought he could get them close enough to Samuel Bell, he'd send an assassin instead.

Hell, he probably had already. On a night like this, it would be exactly what everyone was expecting. They wouldn't have been looking out for people to sneak in and fuck up their computer.

"That's what I'm hoping," Mannix said. "The four of us are going to get noticed. We'll get the appreciation we deserve. And with it, more responsibility."

"Do you think I could get a bigger workshop?" My vision blurred as I imagined my ideal space. It would be three or four times the size of what I have now. Enough space to work with several different people. I might even bring in an apprentice. Maybe Kennedy. I had a feeling she'd get a kick out of it way more than she realised.

Just thinking about her using the pliers on Frank Nixon made my cock hard. Thinking about Kennedy doing pretty much anything made my cock turn to stone. I would have liked more time in Bell's office, so I could fuck her mouth. Oh well, there'd be time for that later.

"I don't see why not," Mannix said.

I fist pumped the air. "Hell yeah. I'm going to need a bath. A big one."

"Feeling dirty?" Ares asked.

I frowned at him and stepped carefully around a bike some kid left out the front of their house. They'd be lucky if it was still there in the morning and not stolen.

"Not for me," I said once I figured out what he was getting at. "I'd put acid in it and then feet or hands. While they're attached to the person—"

"All right, all right, I get it," Ares said hastily. As if he wouldn't be there to watch and enjoy it along with the rest of us.

Kennedy looked up at me. "Acid? That sounds..."

"Exciting?" I suggested. "Arousing? Hot as fuck? Fun?"

She exhaled half a breath. "Something like that, yeah." She let out the other half of her breath with the last word.

I squeezed her hand. "I knew you were the woman for me. Most of the girls I know would be grossed out. Or at least find it weird."

"I'm not most girls," she said.

I remembered the way she let Mannix fuck her on Samuel Bell's desk not even half an hour ago and grinned. "You certainly aren't."

"None of you are like most guys either," she said.

"Don't you fucking forget it," Ares growled.

"As if you'd let me," she retorted. "You in particular are very good at reminding me every chance you get."

"Ares only does it to remind himself. He has a fragile ego." I grinned as he flipped me off.

"Fragile ego, my ass," Kennedy said.

Of course, that was the perfect excuse to squeeze her beautiful ass. Not that I needed one, but I took it anyway. Her butt was perfectly round and firm. Exactly what you'd expect from a gymnast. I could happily keep my hand there forever, or slip it down her crack to toy with her rear hole. I wanted to lube her up and fuck her there. My balls ached at the thought of it. I was the first to fuck her pussy and her mouth, so why not her ass too? If that was greedy, I didn't care. When it came to her, I wanted all her firsts and her lasts, and as much in between as I could get my hand, mouth and cock on or into.

As I squeezed her tender flesh, I noticed Mannix looking back over his shoulder at Bell's house.

"You good?" I asked. I resisted the urge to look back too. Nothing said we were up to bad shit like glancing over our shoulders every few seconds. We were supposed to be playing it cool, so if anyone went past, they didn't pay us any attention.

His expression was a rare display of uncertainty. "I don't know. I don't trust Lila Bell and everything else seemed way too easy."

"It wasn't easy, it was executed exactly as

planned," Ares said. "By you, in case you forgot. Now who has the fragile ego?"

"Still you," Mannix said easily. "My instincts tell me—"

The front of the Bell house lit up brighter than a Christmas tree.

"Fuck."

CHAPTER TWENTY-ONE

Someone shouted, "Over there!"

That was immediately followed by a flood of people pouring out the front gates. Were those guns in their hands?

I decided not to stick around and find out. I kicked off my heels and ran, the guys all around me.

Those were definitely gunshots that slammed into the grass and sidewalk around us.

How the hell they missed us, I had no idea. I very much doubted those were intended to be warning shots. Whether they knew who we were or what we did, they were aiming with intent. Whether that intent was to kill or to injure so they could catch us, I had no idea about that either.

Frankly, I didn't want to find out. I didn't like either of those options.

"Come on. We're out of range, but not for long." Mannix waved us all forward, his expression steely calm. Reassuringly so.

"Especially if they have a rocket launcher," Ice said.

Without glancing over at him I said, "Is that likely?"

"Actually, yes. Bell has an arsenal of all sorts of shit. It's unlikely he or any of his people could get it out and operational this quickly though."

"That's good to know." It was. I suspected a rocket launcher would give us a very unfair disadvantage. Not to mention make a mess out of the streets of Sydney.

"Come on, Princess." Mannix grabbed my hand. We weaved back and forth as we ran to the car and around to the other side of it.

"Get in," he urged. He yanked the back door open and gave me a shove. At the same time, he reached into the foot well and grabbed out three guns. He tossed two to Ares and Ice.

I scrambled inside and stayed down low, while the guys positioned themselves at the front and back of the car. The driver joined Ares near the back, his own gun in his hand.

"Stay down out of sight," Mannix ordered, waving at me to duck down as small as I could. "Don't freak out. We've got you. I promise." He left the door open but moved away.

I hated not being able to see anything, but I hated the idea of being shot even more, so I did what I was told. As for not freaking out, I couldn't make any guarantees.

There was a very real and painful possibility we might all die right here on the streets of one of the most affluent parts of Sydney. What would the news have to say about us?

Oh, right. Nothing. The Bell family or the Brantleys, or even Leo, would pay a shit load of money to cover the whole thing up. By the time they were done, the people living on the street would believe they imagined the entire thing. Or they'd be paid well enough to forget.

Something hit the side of the car and pinged. Bullets, I winced. Each one made a dent that cracked the plastic interior without passing all the way through.

Yet.

I looked up through the window as Ares took

aim. His long fingers twitched as he pulled the trigger. His face was a study in concentration and determination. If this wasn't so scary, it would be hot.

Okay, who was I kidding? It was definitely hot. He knew what to do with that gun and he wouldn't hesitate to kill any of the people coming after us. None of the guys would hesitate. Hell, for all I knew this wasn't their first shootout. Maybe not even their thirteenth. They might be a regular occurrence in the life of Mannix, Ice and Ares. If I was ever going to reconsider my life choices, it would be right now.

It's a bit late for that, I told myself. I was curled up in the footwell of the car that was being shot at. And it was basically my fault, because I was the one who came up with the idea of putting a virus on Bell's computer in the first place.

Had they found it already? Or had Lila Bell and the Brantley twins betrayed us? If I died without knowing the answer to that, I'd be pissed off.

I shifted around to get comfortable. My hand brushed past something hard and cold. I felt around until I curled my fingers around the cool steel.

Another gun.

I'd never used one, but how difficult could it be? I hated the idea of being vulnerable and I didn't want to be a sitting duck or a damsel in distress.

I wanted to be one of them, by their side no matter what. I wasn't just a nerd girl who did gymnastics in her spare time. I was a badass nerd girl who belonged to these three beautiful guys. None of us were going down without a fight.

Unless you're talking about the good kind of going down, which right now I wasn't. That could come later. And so would we.

Yeah, nerves were jumbling my thoughts, but I snatched up the gun and slipped back out of the car.

The road was rough under my feet, cracked and broken, even in this part of the city. Part of me regretted kicking off my heels, but I couldn't have run as fast in them anyway.

I'd suffer the discomfort for a little while. It was better than being dead.

"Beautiful Kennedy, what are you doing?" Ice asked without so much as looking at me.

"I thought I'd help." I moved over beside him, my head and body low, and looked out over the street. At least a dozen people were headed our way, each moving slowly and carefully. They had us outnumbered, but we had a car to hide behind. Surely that meant we were in a good place. Right?

Yeah okay, I'm not that naïve, but it was a better barricade than none. Wishing for an armoured tank right now wouldn't make one appear.

"Give me that." Ice grabbed the gun out of my hand.

Before I could protest he said, "The safety is still on." He clicked something and handed the gun back. "Remember to aim it at the bad guys. That's anyone who isn't us."

"Thanks." That would have made me look silly. Aiming and firing and having nothing come out the other end. That would be almost as useful as bringing a knife to a gunfight.

His teeth flashed white in the darkness. "Any time." He turned and aimed. His shot was quickly followed by a grunt and a thud of someone hitting the ground.

"Shooting people is so impersonal," he complained. "Really not my style at all." He aimed and struck his target again. "At least they could give me a scream of pain or something. Anything."

I suspected he'd happily shoot them all in the knees and take them back to his workshop for a few days.

He ducked down as a bullet passed low over our heads, narrowly missing both of us.

"Now it's personal," he said.

"It wasn't personal before?" I asked.

"Not as much as it is now." He flashed me a smile and got off another shot. A male voice cried out in pain as the bullet took him in the wrist. The next took him in the chest.

"Better them than us," Mannix said. He took out two in quick succession, then dropped down lower.

As far as I could tell, they were coming slower now, and were down to about six or seven. The guys and the driver had killed or maimed at least five potential attackers.

Yeah, this definitely wasn't their first shootout. They knew exactly what they were doing. Did they learn this as boys or at university?

Finally, a university that taught practical skills. Of course, shooting people was only a practical skill in certain occupations and lifestyles, like ours. It probably shouldn't go mainstream.

A bullet, or three, slammed into the window on the opposite side of the car, cracking but not shattering it. Another couple of shots took out the tyres on the other side.

"Well, that sucks," Ice said. "We'll have to find another car so we can get out of here." He didn't sound too concerned.

He leaned in and whispered in my ear. "Over to

the left, there's a tree. The man crouched beside it thinks we don't know he's there. I'm going to draw him out. If you aim low, you can't miss him."

That was a hell of an assumption, but I nodded.

"I can try."

"You've got this." He gave me a quick kiss that was full of the promise of a lot more.

We just had to survive this first. No pressure.

Ice took a few steps to the side and spoke loudly. "I think that's the—"

The man beside the tree rose, gun in hand. All of his attention was on Ice. That was his last mistake.

I took aim and squeezed the trigger. The recoil almost made me squeal in surprise, but the bullet caught the man in the right side of his chest. It was enough to give Ice time to shoot him in the left side of his chest, killing him.

The man staggered a few steps before he fell heavily to the ground and lay very still. The street lights shone off a puddle of blood that snaked out beside him and slowly grew.

Ice stepped back over to me and offered me a high five. "What a team."

I slapped his hand half heartedly and leaned against the car for a moment to catch my breath. The moment I picked up the gun I knew there was a possibility I would kill someone, or take part in killing someone, but doing it... That was another thing.

I wasn't sure if I'd get used to it, or even if I wanted to, but I couldn't let it get to me right now. If I let myself be distracted for too long, that could be exactly what they needed to end me.

"You did good, Firecracker," Ares said. He didn't look at me so he couldn't see my surprise, but he nodded, so he must have known I glanced at him. His expression gave away nothing, but for once he wasn't sneering. His focus hadn't dropped for a moment. Eyes as intense as ever, he watched the street for movement, the gun moving as he tried to pin down a target.

"Thanks," I muttered. I pulled myself together and stood back up again. I could do this. I had to. It was them or us and I was damned if it was going to be us. I was going to protect my guys the way they protected me.

Us against the rest of the world.

"Let's finish this," Mannix said. He moved to the side, almost out from behind the car, gun held in both hands. He aimed but missed. I couldn't even see what he was aiming at.

Another shot hit the side of the car, near the fuel tank.

"Someone thinks this is a movie," Ice said derisively. "The fuel tank isn't going to explode unless—Fuck." He grabbed my hand and yanked me down the street.

The pavement bit into my feet, but I glanced back to see a shadow flick open a cigarette lighter and throw it in the direction of the car.

At first, nothing happened. Then the first trickle from the ruptured fuel tank touched the road and dribbled towards the lighter. The moment they met, the liquid caught fire. It flashed and burnt high enough to reach the fuel tank.

It ignited the fuel around the outside of it, then the fuel inside the car.

Ice shoved me down onto the pavement and threw his body over mine as the car exploded.

CHAPTER TWENTY-TWO

KENNEDY

My face hit the road. I grunted in pain as I grazed my cheek and the side of my chin.

I screwed my eyes shut and threw my arms over my head. A rush of heat poured over us, accompanied by shards of metal and glass. Bits of car rained down on us.

My ears rang from the sound of the explosion, but somewhere in the back of my mind I acknowledged the fact that I was somehow still alive.

Ice's breath in my ear confirmed he was too.

What about Mannix and Ares?

My heart raced. I was sweating profusely. All I could do was lie still and wait.

It would suck to make it this far only to stand up

too soon and get hit by a flying engine. Okay, a smaller car part was much more likely, but that would suck just as hard.

"Beautiful?" Ice murmured. "You okay?"

"Yeah. You?" My eyes felt glued shut, but I managed to force them open. The road looked like a war zone. Bits of car were scattered everywhere. The road where it sat was singed black. Most of the cars around it were smashed up. Shattered windscreens, blasted paint, deep dents.

Fuck.

"Kinda." He peeled himself up off me and looked around, dazed. "We need to get out of here."

"You're hurt." His suit jacket and shirt were in shreds. Where the fabric was torn, he was bleeding.

He glanced down and grinned. "I'm going to have some epic fucking scars. But we really need to get out of here, or we won't live to see them."

Who else but him would be impressed by being injured?

He pushed himself to his feet and gripped my arm to pull me to mine.

My ears still rang, making balancing a challenge.

"Ares and Mannix..."

"They'll find us." He slid his hand down my arm

to lace his fingers in mine and pull me away from the wreckage.

At some point, I'd lost the gun, but I still had my phone and the USB stick in my hand. I would have preferred the gun right now.

We staggered a few metres until we reached the grass. It wasn't until we hit the softer surface that I realised how sore my feet were. They were bleeding too.

I paused and leaned against Ice long enough to tug a piece of metal out of my ankle. I winced as it slid free and reminded myself to get a tetanus shot when I got the chance.

I glanced back over my shoulder to see upright shadows moving towards the site of the explosion. Fuel on the road still burned, the smoke made the shapes dance and writhe like ghosts. They must have stood back when the car blew up, but now they were searching for us again.

I saw no sign of Mannix or Ares.

We retreated into the shadow of a few trees and stopped to catch our breath. Sirens wailed in the distance. They quickly drew closer.

"We need to be away from here before the cops come," Ice said. "They'll have too many questions we don't want to answer."

"Are you sure?" I searched for his eyes in the darkness. "We're the innocent victims in a case of attempted murder."

He laughed softly. "Victims, yes. Innocent, not so much. It's better if they don't know we were here. They'll call it an accident and move on. That's what we need to do." He tugged my hand and we slipped further away.

"Right now, Samuel Bell won't be sure who we are, or who fucked with his computer. If the police detain us, then he'll know. And we can't be sure if any of them are on his payroll."

"I hadn't thought of that," I admitted. He was right. All of that would be bad.

"Lucky you have the Iceman around." He flashed me a brief smile, one that spoke of the pain he was in.

"Do you need to rest for a minute?" I asked. It was too dark to get a real idea of how badly injured he was, but it must be pretty bad if he was showing any sign of it. If he let it get past his laid-back exterior.

"Nah, I'm fine." He sounded dismissive, but not entirely convincing. "If we weren't in a hurry, I'd pin you to a tree and fuck you silly."

I suspected he thought about doing that anyway,

but the sirens were closer now, and the voices behind us louder and more insistent.

"They can't be far. Spread out and look."

"I guess they didn't find Mannix or Ares yet," Ice remarked. He was walking faster now, all but dragging me with him.

I had to trot to keep up, which hurt the hell out of my feet. I pushed the pain aside as best I could and kept going. The thought of being caught by Bell, or sidetracked by the cops, was a good incentive to keep putting one foot in front of the other. The further and faster we went, the harder it became to ignore it.

After a while, it swamped my thoughts. All I knew was pain and moving forward, step by step. I couldn't even say how fast I was going or where we were. Pain encompassed everything.

Tears blurred my vision and trickled down my cheeks, but I didn't slow.

Not until Ice came to a sudden stop.

"Long time no see," one of the twins drawled.

I blinked to clear my eyes. I thought it might have been Hunter, but I wasn't sure until he spoke again.

"Parker was just saying he wondered if you were inside the car when it blew up. I guess not."

"We're not that easy to kill," Ice bragged.

Parker turned on the light on his watch and waved it up and down at us quickly before turning it off.

"Maybe not, but you look like shit. And it sounds like we should vacate the area pretty fucking quickly."

"That's what we were trying to do, bro," Ice told him.

"Lucky you bumped into us then," Hunter said. "Come on, we'll give you a hand." He slipped an arm around me. We made it a few steps before he realised I wasn't keeping up.

"My feet," I whispered. I didn't want to make a fuss, but I also didn't want to slow us down. I'd feel like crap if we all got caught because of me.

"Piece of cake," he said cheerfully. He leaned down and placed his arm under my knees, the other under my arm and swept me up.

"The fuck?" Ice growled.

"Chillax, dude," Hunter said. "Your girl is hurt and you're in no shape to carry her. Parker and I can always leave you here if you prefer."

"No," I said quickly. "It's okay. Hunter is helping me, nothing else."

Ice groused under his breath, but trudged behind

us. Hopefully he wasn't thinking of chaining them in his workroom and doing things to the twins because one of them dared to touch me.

Under any other scenario it was okay, but in this case, without Hunter's help, I'd be fucked. I wondered why the guys called them the evil twins. They seemed nice enough to me.

I leaned my head against Hunter's chest and tried to keep my eyes open. He was at least as hard as the other guys, although he was younger than me. Not by much, but by enough. Even if they didn't have a girlfriend, I wasn't even slightly interested in either twin. They were attractive, and ripped, but they weren't my guys.

Besides, I had my hands full with three. I didn't need five boyfriends.

"So you managed to piss off old man Bell, huh?" Hunter asked.

"I guess so," I said noncommittally. "I get the impression that isn't difficult to do."

"Not even a little bit difficult," he agreed. "He's even more high strung then our brother, Reuben. Samuel Bell kills people if they look at him the wrong way. Reuben just puts them on his shit list and makes their life hell. If he can be bothered with them. Mostly, doing that is a waste of money and resources. I guess that's why Bell kills people. It's cheaper."

I hadn't expected to get a crash course in mobster economics 101, but he had a point. Killing people was probably a lot cheaper than what Ice did to them in his workroom. I knew if I suggested that, he'd reply that it wasn't as much fun.

Sometimes saving money wasn't everything.

"What did you do to piss him off?" Parker asked.

"You don't want to know," Ice told him. "If only because someone is going to ask sooner or later and you won't have to lie if you don't know."

"What makes you think we have a problem with lying?" Hunter glanced over to Ice.

"Absolutely nothing," Ice said. "In this case you're better off not knowing and I'm not going to tell you anyway, so this conversation is basically moot."

Hunter shrugged, making me rise and fall in his arms. "Suit yourself."

After a moment he spoke again. "You weren't sent to assassinate Bell, were you? Because if you were, you are the least stealthy assassins we've ever seen. Right Parker?"

"Exactly," Parker agreed. "Hunter and I are stealthier than you."

"Wait a minute, Park." Hunter looked over at him. "Are you suggesting we're not stealthy?"

"I mean, we could be if we wanted to, but we're usually not called on to sneak around."

"That's true," Hunter conceded. "But when we sneak, no one sees us coming. Like that time with Penn, Wolf Venom's keyboardist."

Parker grinned. "Yeah, that was awesome. He had no idea until we... We shouldn't tell you about that. If you're not going to share, then neither will we."

"I don't think I want to know," I admitted. The band's keyboard player had a reputation for being an asshole, but he was a gifted musician. I was content only knowing him for his music and not anything that went on behind the scenes. If they wanted to tell me a few stories about Zeke, then I'd listen.

It dawned on me I was being carried by the brother of none other than Zeke Brantley, my favourite singer in the whole wide world. Holy shit. This might be the closest I ever got to him, and I wouldn't be able to tell anyone about it.

Figured.

"You probably don't, but it was awesome. Trust me on that." Hunter smiled down at me. He was the kind of guy who was too good-looking for his own good or anyone else's. I bet he got away with all sorts of shit he shouldn't. That might be why the guys called them the evil twins, because they did things just because they could. If that made them evil, then what were we? Killing people wasn't exactly something nice people did, was it?

The sirens were almost deafening now. Everyone within a five or six block radius would hear them.

We ducked in behind a fence as flashing lights came screaming around the corner. Two police cars and an ambulance, followed by a fire truck flew past us toward the scene of the explosion.

People started to step out of their homes, bolder now the authorities were here.

We stayed crouched down for several minutes, or approximately three million rapid heartbeats.

"I don't think they saw us," Parker said. "If anyone was coming after you, they would have scattered by now."

I would have been relieved if I knew where Mannix and Ares were. They were okay, they had to be. If they weren't... My heart wrenched at the idea.

"Okay, let's keep going," Hunter said.

We were about to step out of the darkest

shadows when we were all illuminated by the light of a phone.

"There you are," Lila Bell said lightly. "Good work. Daddy will be pleased."

CHAPTER TWENTY-THREE

Shit.

For half a second, I thought she was joking. That she'd help the twins to help us get away. She was dating them after all, wasn't she? Did that mean she wanted the same peace they did?

A glance at Hunter's face showed he thought the same thing. Then the cogs and wheels in his mind turned. I saw that too.

Along with the exact moment Ice and I were fucked.

"We figured you'd be around here somewhere," Hunter said lightly. "Parker was just saying you couldn't be far away. Weren't you Parker?"

"Yeah." Parker cottoned on to what Hunter was

saying. "We were trying to find you while staying out of sight, in case your dad's men mistook us for these two." He jerked his thumb towards Ice and I. "We found them lurking back there and figured we'd bring them to you."

My whole body stiffened. Fucking motherfucker. So much for helping us. I should have known they couldn't be trusted. What part of 'evil twins' did I forget to pay attention to? Just because they seemed nice, didn't mean they were.

And now we were screwed.

"Where are the other two?" Lila fixed one then the other with a firm look. If it wasn't obvious before who was in charge here, it was now. Not the twins. She couldn't have been more than eighteen, but she clearly had them pussy whipped.

"We haven't seen them," Hunter said. "We can take these two to your father then go out looking again." He made it sound like he was going out for ice cream, or more alcohol when the party was at risk of running out. Not looking for my guys to hand them over to their enemy.

Now I wondered what they did to Wolf Venom's keyboard player, because they seemed to be lacking a conscience. If they'd hand over their allies to their enemies, they were shitheads to say the least.

The look Ice gave them lived up to his name. For once, he wasn't smiling. He was mentally cutting small strips of skin from each twin. Or tearing off their toenails before breaking every bone in their body. He was listening to them scream and beg for mercy or death. He was watching them dangle from the ceiling by their wrists, their feet centimetres from the floor, hungry and without water for days. Or with just enough water to keep them alive while he worked on them a bit more.

I was glad he had something to console himself with, because all I had was my anger. Of that, I had plenty. I would have cheerfully used the pliers on either of the twins. I could start with the balls and go from there. Okay, thinking violent thoughts was helpful to a limited extent. The realisation I couldn't do anything to them increased my anger.

"Put me down," I hissed.

Hunter looked down at me and cocked his head. "I don't think so. I think if I do that, you'll try to run. You'll only end up hurting yourself if you do that." His tone was perfectly reasonable and conversational, and accompanied by an expression that was borderline giving a shit. Or would be if I bought even a little bit of it.

"Now you care," I said sarcastically. The asshole

and his asshole brother threw us under the bus, right at his precious, fucking girlfriend. What a pair of suck-ups.

Ares would have made some snide remark about Lila having a gold plated pussy, or one that contracts back to virgin tightness after she's fucked. Something that would make them hand us over to her and her father. Maybe they were fucking Samuel Bell too.

Whatever, I didn't give a shit if they both sucked him off every night. Or each other for that matter.

Okay, I didn't think about that too deeply, because that was way hotter than it should have been. The very last thing I needed, or wanted, was to be turned on by these asshole twins.

"Of course I care," Hunter said. "We've been looking for a peace offering for a while now, and you two are perfect. Bell will be happy, and Reuben, he'll pretend he never heard of any of you."

He turned to Ice and said, "What is it they call you three? The Devils of Dusk Bay? Personally, I've always thought that was an over-exaggeration, but either way, it's a point in our favour. Leo might even be happy to be rid of you."

Leo might start pulling off heads if anything happened to his son. As for the rest of us, I wasn't convinced he'd give a shit. At least my mother would miss me. And the kids at the gym.

"Who calls us that?" Ice asked. "Because that's a cooler nickname than the evil fucking twins."

His gaze slid off Hunter, over to Lila. "What do they call you and your sister? The other evil twins? I know, the twisted, no, *wicked* sisters. That has a ring to it, don't you think?"

I didn't see she had a gun in her hand until she raised it.

"I think I'm the one calling the shots." Her tone was colder than Antarctica. "Take them inside. We'll try to bypass the circus the idiot neighbours called in."

She made a face like she'd just swallowed a glass of lemon juice. Evidently dead people and an explosion was an inconvenience to someone like her. Heaven forbid she got a bit of someone's brain on the bottom of her shoe. I wouldn't mind having her brain on the bottom of my shoe. If I was wearing shoes.

"Let me guess, you're the evil twin out of you and your sister," I said. I tried not to flinch when she turned the gun on me.

She gave me a look like I shouldn't goad her, but said, "I'd kill you now and get it over with, but I know who you are and what you did. You're the only one who can undo it."

That was assuming a lot, but I had the sense to keep my mouth shut. Even if I couldn't undo the virus, it might be the only thing keeping me alive right now. As long as they thought I could do it, I might stand half a chance of finding a way out. It wasn't much of a life ring, but I'd cling to it for as long as I could.

"For the record, if you kill him, I won't help you." I nodded toward Ice. "That goes for if you maim or injure him in any way." Just in case they thought there was a loophole in there somewhere.

She looked as though she might kill him anyway, but then she nodded and waved for the twins to walk ahead of her.

Did she not trust them to walk behind her? I wasn't sure I could blame her if she didn't. I didn't trust them as far as I could spit.

I hated the fact Hunter had to carry me, but I was grateful for two things. Firstly, that I wasn't draped over his shoulder like a sack of potatoes. And secondly, that it let my feet rest and gave me time to think. I needed to keep my eye out for Mannix and Ares, and an opportunity to escape. I managed to get myself out of Leo's fortress, I could get myself away from Bell's. Ice and I would find a way.

We skirted around the police who started to set up a perimeter around the wreckage. The firetruck was still there, but the fire was out. The road was now covered in foam.

In front of the ambulance, several bodies were laid out, all of their faces covered. A couple of police officers carried another one over and set it beside the others. I recognised the driver of the car who brought us here only an hour or two ago.

If he hadn't made it, then...

My breath caught in my throat, but I couldn't let myself think about the possibilities the guys didn't survive. They did. They *had* to. They were out there somewhere, hiding or looking for me. They might be injured, but they weren't dead. I wouldn't allow them to be dead. I didn't give a fuck if it didn't work that way. They were alive because I said they were.

That was what I told myself anyway, over and over. Whatever it took to hang onto my sanity.

I glanced up at Hunter, but his eyes looked straight ahead. What the fuck was his agenda, really? He claimed he wanted peace between the families and maybe this would achieve it. And maybe it wouldn't. There was a distinct possibility that all he was doing was taking us to our deaths. Wasn't he supposed to be an ally?

I considered the possibility he was playing Lila Bell, but I doubted it. Both twins seemed to genuinely care about her. Why, I had no idea. Maybe because love was blind, hearing-impaired and not entirely sane. I only had to look at my relationship with the guys to realise that.

Wait a minute. Had the word love snuck into my brain?

Yeah. Yes it had. I cared about them, but until now I hadn't thought any further than that. It made sense though. None of us had any intention of letting the others go. What else would that be but love? A twisted, crazy kind of love, but still love.

He must have realised I was looking at him, because Hunter glanced down at me and smiled.

Ares would have been proud of the glare I gave him in return. I even managed to curl my lip. Go me.

Hunter smirked. Of course he would, he was holding all the cards.

"I know you haven't been around Mannix and the other guys for that long," he said slowly. "Long enough that they've managed to suck you into some crazy shit. But not long enough that you can't get yourself out of it if you want to."

"How would I do that?" I asked as if I was actually interested.

"I'm sure you'll think of something," he said. He glanced back at Lila, a hint of uncertainty on his face. It occurred to me maybe he had no idea why her father was after us, and what I could fix for him.

Hunter was clutching at straws, but while he was doing that he gave me an idea. Was it a good idea? I didn't have a clue. It might be. It might backfire in my face.

"Right," I said softly. I closed my eyes and tried to ignore the fact we were walking toward the gate leading into Bell's house. I considered shouting out to the police for help, but I bit my lip instead.

As Ice said, they would have a lot of questions and I didn't have all the answers. Added to that, the street was full of innocent people now, and Lila had a gun. There was no doubt in my mind she'd use it on someone to punish me for crying out. She seemed like the sadistic kind. Much more so than Ice. He tortured people for fun, but they weren't innocent people. That was an important distinction.

Ice walked beside us with a stiff back. Every so often he'd glare at one twin or the other, all over his shoulder, but mostly his eyes were on or around me like a bodyguard. He would have preferred to be the one carrying me, I saw that in his body language, along with the fact he was still in pain.

We stepped through the gate and my heart sank further. We were caught in the spider's web and I had no idea if we would ever get out again.

CHAPTER TWENTY-FOUR

Security guards fell in around us when we passed through the gate. Lila didn't even have to say a word. We went from a gun on us to several.

What felt like a death march, we went up the brightly illuminated driveway and back into the house.

"This is nice," Ice said as though we never stepped foot in the place. "It could use a little more red."

No one answered him. I gave him a glance to suggest he not provoke anyone, but Ice was going to be Ice. He almost seemed to be enjoying himself. No one said he was completely sane.

We were taken to the office. It felt like days ago Mannix fucked me on the desk which Samuel Bell now sat behind. It had to be him, because no one else would dare to sit there. The resemblance to Lila was obvious. They both had dark hair and eyes that seemed to see right through me. He looked as though he could eviscerate my soul with a glance.

I managed to hold his gaze without wavering. I wasn't going to show any sign of fear or weakness. The moment I did, he'd exploit it. Still, it was difficult to avoid being intimidated. He was clearly used to getting exactly what he wanted when he wanted. He reminded me of Mannix, Ares and Leo. Ruthless, determined and powerful.

Right now, he held all the cards.

He turned his gaze to the evil twins and his frown noticeably increased in depth.

"Hunter and Parker helped us catch these two," Lila said quickly. For the first time, she seemed slightly rattled. Only slightly. Her chin was still raised, defiant. "She's the one who put the virus in the computer."

"Are you certain of that?" Samuel Bell spoke for the first time. His voice was deep, gravelly.

Now Lila seemed uncertain. "Do you know who she is—"

"I know precisely who she is." His voice was low, but she stopped speaking the moment he started.

"Kennedy Knight. Stepdaughter of Leo Cassani. Computer science major. Gymnastics coach and owner of her own gym." He nodded for Hunter to put me down.

Thankfully the flooring under my feet was carpet, and I managed to contain a wince.

"Then you know I'm harmless," I said. "I was in the wrong place at the wrong time. If you don't mind, we'll get out of your hair." I gestured to Ice.

Bell ignored me and turned to Ice. "Isaac Miller. You have an interesting reputation yourself."

Ice grinned. "Thanks. I try. It would suck if anyone thought I was boring."

That was something no one could ever accuse him of being.

Bell looked unamused. He turned back to me. "If I hadn't needed a file tonight, that virus might have gone unnoticed." He looked at his screen and nodded. "I can see it at work. Deleting my files and corrupting my system. Can it be undone?"

I considered how to answer that. In the end I decided on honesty.

"Yes. And also no. I can stop it from making things worse, or deleting anything else. It may be possible to recover some, even most of the deleted files, but it would take time. And someone who knew what they were doing."

"You," he stated.

I shrugged. "I know how the virus works. I could disable it faster than anyone else." I was banking on him believing me. Other people might be able to fix it faster, but unless they were on the premises, it would take precious time to get them here. I was his best bet. If I was inclined to help him.

He nodded. "Do it." He looked past Lila to one of his security guards. "Take Mr. Miller downstairs. See to his injuries, but restrain him."

He returned his dark gaze to me. "You understand what happens to him is up to you. One toe out of line and he'll lose one of his feet. Try to screw me over and he'll be missing other, vital body parts. He'll wish he was dead."

Any normal person would be scared at being threatened like that, but not Ice. He was actually grinning. Only he would be excited at the prospect of being tortured and mutilated. I was almost certain he wasn't putting on an act so I'd feel less pressured and scared. He was still smiling as he was led from the room.

"I understand," I said evenly. "I'm going to need access to your computer."

Bell stood and gestured for me to sit in his chair.

I grimaced at the warmth as I sat, but leaned forward and focused my attention on the screen. The virus worked faster than I anticipated. If I had to guess, I'd say at least thirty percent of his files were toast.

"Yeah, this might take longer than I thought."

Bell placed his palms on the desk and leaned over towards me. "For every hour, Mr Miller loses a toe. When he has no more, we'll start on his fingers."

I looked up at him. He wasn't going to let us walk out of here alive. I knew that with absolute certainty. Hunter was right when he said Mannix's family, and the Brantleys, would pretend we didn't exist. We'd be lucky if we had something as fancy as a shallow grave.

"I've stopped the virus from doing more damage, but the time it takes to undo what it's done is what is going to take," I said, reasonably. "Threats aren't going to make it any quicker. I'm not even sure if I *can* undo it."

"Find out," he snapped. He straightened up and paced across the room, past his daughter and the twins.

I gave Hunter and Parker a dirty look. Neither asshole had the grace to look regretful or even embarrassed. If anything, all they looked was nervous. Of course, they were in the spider's web as deeply as I was.

"If Ice runs out of toes, you can always take theirs." I nodded towards them and gave them both a look of pure venom.

Lila cut me a matching look. I think she would have shot me then and there if she was allowed to. The feeling was mutual.

I smiled sarcastically at her, then turned my gaze back to the screen. She was the bitch who made this bed, she could lie in it with them. I wouldn't lose any sleep over either of the twins being tortured. In fact, the thought cheered me up.

I pinched the bridge of my nose and skimmed through a bunch of files and directories. There were a lot of them left, which contributed to the computer being slow. Or at least, slower than it could have been. If it was anyone but Bell, I'd offer to help expand its memory.

"We are just going back out to find the other two who were with her and her boyfriend," Lila said. She stepped toward the door clearly expecting to be stopped, but wanting to be gone from there as quickly as possible.

"Mannix and Ares," Parker supplied helpfully. "Leo's son and one of his friends."

I made a note that, if I survived this, I'd hack the twins' bank accounts and send all their money to a worthy cause. Maybe a charity for homeless people.

In spite of the guys' warning not to hack into Brutham Academy systems, I was tempted to do that too. I could give them both a failing grade and get them kicked out.

People often underestimated how much power a vengeful nerd actually had. Especially one who was good with computers. The things I could fuck with... It was a long and ugly list. Or beautiful, depending on your perspective.

"I'll send some people after them," Bell said. "You go upstairs to your room. You two, get out of my house. If I see you back here, you can join Mr. Miller downstairs. If you so much as think about my daughter again, you'll regret the day were born."

When I looked back up, the room was empty except for me, Bell and one of his men who still had a gun held in his hand.

"You know they're not going to stop seeing each other, don't you? Teenage rebellion and all that." I shrugged one shoulder. I wasn't trying to provoke him, not really. If it gave the incentive for some sort of vendetta against the twins, then I was all for fuelling that fire. I hadn't realised I had such a capacity for holding a grudge, but apparently I did. It was always good to learn these things about yourself.

Oh, he knew all right. Even though his face was as composed as ever, it was right there in his eyes. Along with the knowledge if he had the twins killed, his daughter would never speak to him again. I got that, I wouldn't speak to my mother if she had the guys killed. Although, my guys were worth a thousand of the twins.

"Can you fix it?" he snapped. His patience was becoming threadbare, but it still wouldn't get this done any faster.

I looked back down and let my fingers race across the keyboard. "I've recovered about ten percent of your files." Surprisingly, none of it seemed to be porn.

"I should be able to recover another ten to fifteen percent, but at least five to ten percent is gone permanently."

He growled under his breath. "Can you tell what's gone?"

"Only the empty directory names of one or two," I admitted. "One titled *Hammer* is empty. Another one just called *four-five-sevenx*, is also gone. Other-wise it's just... Gone."

It could have been anything from his plan for world domination, to photos of his precious daughters. Hell, for all I knew it was a menu from his favourite restaurant. The only way to tell was if he looked for himself and remembered what he had and where he had it.

He looked pissed. More so than he already had. "Recover what you can."

My heart raced and a feeling of dread settled over me. I was sitting in the eye of the storm and whatever was coming was going to be a shit load worse than this. If I was lucky, I'd be dead in a couple of hours. If I wasn't lucky, I would wish I was dead in a couple of hours.

My hands hovered over the keys. If I was dead anyway, then shouldn't I do what I came here to do? If I didn't, then what was the point of all of this? Mannix and Ares were probably long gone by now. This way, they'd have something to show for coming here in the first place. That might be enough to make up for losing Ice and me.

My palms were sweaty and my fingers trembled. I considered negotiating but knew there was no way we'd get any concessions from Samuel Bell. Even if I threatened him, he wasn't going to let Ice leave.

Nothing and no one was going to save us.

I looked up to see Bell watching me. His otherwise smooth brow was crinkled with a tiny frown. I've never seen someone so in control of his own emotions. His control was tight, but not flawless. Not robotic. He was a guitar string drawn tight. With the right pressure he'd snap. It wouldn't be a violent snap. More like a softly spoken order to kill me. But still a snap.

His chin lifted a fraction in warning. He knew exactly what I was thinking and we both knew what would happen if I ignored that warning.

My eyes still on his, I pressed the button to reactivate the virus and double its speed.

CHAPTER TWENTY-FIVE

KENNEDY

The room was pitch black. Completely devoid of light and sound.

The ground was hard and the walls were dry. That was the only thing I could tell about the space. That and if I walked five steps from any corner, I'd graze my knuckles on the opposite corner. There was no water. No food. No bedding.

Nothing. After I reactivated the virus, I thought he'd kill me immediately.

Instead, he'd nodded to his minion, who took me at gunpoint down a set of stairs at the back of the house. He'd unbolted the door and waved me inside.

I slumped down to the floor as tears trickled down my cheek.

I waited for my eyes to adjust to the darkness,

but they never did. I listened for a sound, any sound, but it didn't come. The silence made my ears ring.

How long would it take before that drove me completely crazy?

That was exactly the point of a room like this. I remembered seeing one when Mum took me to Port Arthur in Tasmania. They sadistically used sensory deprivation rooms to punish inmates and drive them insane. Figures Bell would have one. It might be an understatement to suggest I was regretting my life choices right now. If I hadn't reactivated the virus, he might have killed me by now or at least put me in a room with some light.

Did Ice's workroom have a place like this? If it didn't now, it would if we got out of here and I told him about it. Off the top of my head, I could think of four people I'd put in it.

I sighed and sat back against the wall. Maybe I deserved to be in here, alone in the dark. I learnt a lot about myself since moving to Dusk Bay, and most of it wasn't very nice. I had a darker, more twisted soul than I ever would have suspected. A sadistic side that held onto a grudge with an iron grip.

Formerly innocent, naïve Kennedy Knight was not a nice person.

And I was going to die here.

In the dark.

Without a sound.

Alone.

THANKS FOR READING! The story continues in Trap.

If you'd like a bonus scene of Kennedy, Ice and Mannix in the shower, you can find that here.

ABOUT THE AUTHOR

Maggie Alabaster writes reverse harem and, paranormal, sci-fi and fantasy romance.

She lives in NSW, Australia with one spouse, two daughters, one dog, and countless birds.

Jo Bradley writes contemporary romance.

Sign up for Maggie's newsletter! Sign Up!

Join Maggie's reader group! Join here!

Follow Maggie on Bookbub! Click here to follow me!

Check out Maggie's website- www.maggiealabaster.com

Sign up for Jo's newsletter

Join Jo's reader group Jo Bradley's Book Addicts

Follow Jo on Bookbub

Saving Abbie books 1-4

Saving Abbie books 4-6 + Venomous

Ruthless Claws

Book 1 Ivory

Book 2 Crimson

Book 3 Elodie

Harmony's Magic

Book 1 Summoned by Fire

Book 2 Summoned by Fate

Book 3 Summoned by Desire

Shifter's Vault

Book 1 Discarded

Book 2 Deceived

Book 3 Disgraced

My Alien Mates

Book 1 Star Warriors

Book 2 Star Defenders

Book 3 Star Protectors

Academy of Modern Magic